Buffalo City
Moonshine Murders

Sharron Frink

Don't miss these other great books by Sharron Frink:

- Longview Legacy

- Saving Madison

- Bertie

- Family Protection Act

- Family Protection Act 2: The Seed of Life

- Family Protection Act 3: The Unknown Asset

- Prisoner of Experience

All are available as e-books and print books on amazon.com

Buffalo City Moonshine Murders is a work of fiction

Copyright 2014, Sharron Frink

SharronFrink.com

I'd like to express special thanks to the people who first told me about Buffalo City: John Wallace and Frank Ausband. You fired up my imagination with your enthusiasm and that led to this story!

And my appreciation, as always, to my wonderful husband and First Reader, Rand, who never fails to encourage and support my writing habit.

Also, to Alta, Sherry & Sherry: Well, what can I say? Couldn't have done it without you!

Cover design by Sharron Frink

cover art:

Original oil painting of Ocracoke Island by Alta Steed

Buffalo City Moonshine Murders
is a work of fiction. While built around actual locales,
the events portrayed are all products of the author's
imagination.

Some real places and historical characters are
referred to by their actual names. Any resemblance of
the fictional characters or places to real ones is entirely
coincidental.

Buffalo City actually existed as a town, at one time
the largest town in Dare County, North Carolina.
Today there is nothing left in those woods to indicate
that anyone ever lived there – except the memories of a
few people and some very good tall tales.

Buffalo City

CHAPTER 1

Ocracoke Island, North Carolina

1981

The withered old man moaned, grimaced and then opened his eyes just a slit as he shifted around restlessly in his bed. He gradually became aware that he was alone at last; the nurses, the visitors, and even the family had stepped out of the room. The whisper-like noises of their presence had stopped: the faint, muted conversations and tearful sobbing, the sounds of people trying to move softly about in the room, feet scraping across the linoleum, the thud of them bumping into things and one another. But even that had been enough to keep him painfully semi-conscious.

He looked around to see his bedroom, with things left just the way they had been when his sweet Lillian had passed away. He'd never let them change a thing since that day, despite his fussy daughters always wanting to 'pretty things up'. The memory of his wife Lillian and his hope to see her beautiful face again soon caused a feeling of peace to wash over him, making his pain fade into the background.

He felt his mind drifting away and his body slowly relaxing, each muscle now releasing the tension that it had held onto for so long, the near constant pain of the last few months receding as his mind focused on the last image he would ever think of: an old green wine bottle bobbing around in the water, slowly meandering along, in no hurry to get to where it was going, aimlessly floating, floating, floating… and taking his burden of guilt off across the water with it.

The old fellow felt truly free for the first time in fifty years and he died with a smile on his face, unburdened at last.

Two days later
Near Manteo, North Carolina

The wine bottle flew through the air, spinning end over end until it hit the water with a splash.

"Is that all? Just throw it as far as I can?" the tall, skinny young man asked, scratching his head.

The girl nodded, her long hair blowing around her face in the stiff wind. "That's it. He just asked me to pitch it into the Croatan Sound off the bridge between Manteo and Manns Harbor."

They looked at one another, and she shrugged. "He asked, I promised, and I guess we're done here." She leaned against the rail and looked down across the water.

He shook his head. "I know that you're a hospice nurse but you take your patients way too seriously, Sheila, you know that? We should have just thrown that old thing in the trash! Or off the Bonner Bridge, even, and not come all the way up here to Manteo! It's a long way to drive to do a favor for somebody who's dead!"

She made a face and shook her finger at him. "Listen Troy, you didn't have to come! I just thought that since you have that big strong pitching arm, you could throw it farther than anybody I know!"

The backhanded compliment caused the young man to pull his shoulders up and stand a little straighter; he lifted his hand to shade his eyes and studied the floating bottle. "Well, that's a good hundred feet, and it's bobbin' up and down just fine. Nobody could'a done better, I reckon, what with the wind whippin' round like it is!" He shoved the long, shaggy locks of his mullet haircut back off his face.

Sheila sighed. "Let's go then." She turned, walked off the bridge and headed toward the parked car, grabbing his hand. "The old man never asked much of me, you know, and I liked him. He was easy to take care of and hardly ever complained, even though you could tell that he was hurting real bad there at the end. It was sort of a last request, and it was really all that I could do for him..."

He put his arm around her as they walked. "It's okay, Baby, you did what you promised and now I'm hungry. Let's go get some burgers and fries, okay?"

"You buying this time?" she asked, raising an eyebrow.

He grinned. "Now you know I ain't got no money, Honey, that's why I keep you around!"

She elbowed him in the side. "You are a useless man – if you weren't so good-lookin', I swear I'd drop you like a hot potato!"

He nuzzled her ear. "I'm handy in all kinds of ways, Baby, and you know that!"

She giggled and swatted at him; they walked up to the car.

"What did that paper that was in the bottle say, you think?" he asked, nudging her a little with his elbow.

She gave him a serious look. "I don't know, I didn't read it; I just rolled the pages up real tight, put a rubber band around it and jammed it all in there. Then I put in the cork as far as it would go and sealed it all up with melted candle wax like he told me to do last week. Besides, he must have written it a while back. He's not been able to get around for some time now, that's why he needed home nursing."

"Think it could have been something about a treasure or some such?" Troy wiggled his eyebrows.

Sheila snorted. "Not likely. Virgil was comfortable, but nobody would have considered him rich, just did alright for himself, that's all. No, it was probably some old story; he was always telling me stories about Buffalo City and everything that used to go on there."

"Well, that place has been a ghost town for thirty years at least, so whatever valuables that might have been left there have been well picked over by now by scavengers..."

She nodded. "Yeah, probably. I'm sure it was nothing valuable, just some story he wanted to leave for posterity or something like that." She waved her hand in the air.

"Okay," he said, "you did your duty and that's done, let's go get some supper."

"This'll make a real far-out story to tell our friends, anyway," she said, laughing. They got into her car, drove back toward town and forgot all about the old man and his message in a bottle.

Chapter 2

SARAH'S STORY

****

Outer Banks of North Carolina
Present Day

Sarah's mind was drifting away toward thoughts of an *'apple ugly'* – the biggest, tastiest apple fritter on planet earth and served in a little café not too much further down the road. Sticky fingers pulling off moist, chewy chunks of glazed apple-filled pastry... her mouth watered just thinking about it!

Waaaaahhhhh!!!!!

The sudden loud, blaring sound caused the muscles in Sarah's body to spasm involuntarily and her heart to pound as her multi-tasking mind was snapped back to her driving. She looked around and realized that it was simply the sound of a car horn somewhere nearby. This ridiculous edginess was only one of the minor symptoms of her stress overload: a short fuse, trouble sleeping, headaches and more – she had them all. It was way past time for her to take this vacation!

And when her cell buzzed and vibrated on the seat beside her a few minutes later, she flinched again. She decided to ignore the call. Lowering her car's visor and shifting it to the left to shield her face from the morning sun coming up over the dunes, she frowned a little at the annoying sound, but laughed out loud and then broke out in a big grin.

Whoever it is, they can just wait! I'll call them back when I'm good and ready – or not! she told herself, reaching over to stuff the blasted phone deep inside her large hobo bag. Turning the radio on and tuning it to the nearest oldies station, she rolled down her window and slowed to the legal speed limit, heading south on NC 12, the two lane road to Cape Hatteras and beyond.

No hurry, no worry! Time to sing out loud and dance in the car even if somebody sees me! she thought with a big grin.

She was headed to Ocracoke Island! It was the one place where Sarah felt that she could truly relax – a small island village at the southern end of North Carolina's Outer Banks. Time seemed to move more slowly on Ocracoke, just like the flotsam and jetsam that floated on the surface of the ocean, aimlessly going somewhere – eventually – but in no hurry at all to get there. And she'd be seeing two of her oldest friends who always helped her unwind as nothing else could!

The three of them had planned and taken this annual vacation on Ocracoke together for years now, and every year seemed to be better than the one before. They took turns cooking great meals, hanging out on the beach and riding bikes all over the charming little island. They drank wine at night and played board games or just sat on the porch and talked until they couldn't stay awake any longer. Nobody even turned on the tv – it was a wonderful change from her hectic pace at home!

For the other two women it was really a working vacation; Aleta, the artist, always painted several local scenes and those paintings went straight to the *Down Creek Gallery* on the island, where they sold like hotcakes. She'd lived up in the northern part of the Outer Banks for over thirty years now and her soft style of plein-air painting appealed to locals as well as anyone who had ever vacationed in that area.

Kate, the writer, usually used the vacation as a chance to get work done on a new novel. She'd find a quiet place in the house they rented to set up her computer and spend long hours playing with her imaginary friends in their make-believe worlds. Her novels were fiction, so she could create her characters and then, as she liked to say, "kill 'em off" if and when she pleased. She'd sit writing for hours, and all they'd hear from her was the occasional snicker. Sarah usually figured that the sound of Kate's laughing meant one of the bad guys was getting what he or she deserved!

They were all three 'GRITS', that is, *Girls Raised in the South*, so they laughed at the same things and loved the natural beauty and unchangeable peace and quiet of this tiny windswept island refuge. This girls' week was something they all looked forward to each year.

Before boarding the Hatteras ferry, Sarah had a few stops to make: first, to get a cheeseburger (with everything on it!) at *"Burger, Burger!"* in Avon, the best hamburger place she'd found on the Outer Banks. A burger that was twice as tall as it was wide! Those handmade burgers with the grilled buns were just like she remembered from her childhood – *so good*! And the fries... and the onion rings...

And then she'd hit that little café in Buxton to buy that 'Apple Ugly', hoping they had not sold all of them made for the day. Those things were delicious, sweet and huge; it would take the group a day or two to finish them off!

Then there would be one last stop at the quaint little cottage bookstore, *"Buxton Village Books,"* to visit with the friendly owner Gee Gee, and pick up something new to read while in Ocracoke. Hopefully there would be a new book by a local author... she always enjoyed those. Making these three stops before the ferry had become Sarah's little ritual and always meant a great start to her week.

Sarah feasted on her burger, which was fantastic (but she shouldn't have ordered those yummy sweet potato fries – her stomach was popping!) and she had a nice chat with Chyrel, the owner of the café. A true Outer Banks native born and raised, Chyrel knew all about the area. She was always happy to take a moment, visit with her customers and share a smile or a laugh. Sarah loitered around there for a while after eating, and then made her stops at the bakery and the bookstore along the way before heading south to board the Hatteras/Ocracoke ferry.

The ferry ride from Hatteras to Ocracoke took anywhere from thirty minutes to an hour, depending on where the channel was at the moment. The hurricanes and ever-moving currents caused the sands to shift so much in those shallow waters that the ferry crews had to adjust on a regular basis. Frequently they would have to take the long way around to avoid grounding the ferry on wandering sandbars that would appear suddenly – and then shortly afterward disappear, turning up somewhere else nearby.

You could actually see the north end of Ocracoke Island from the Hatteras ferry dock, so it seemed a bit strange to head out in the opposite direction on the ferry and embark on this strange circuitous route that took such a long time to go such a short distance.

But to Sarah that ferry ride was the real beginning of her vacation. She quite literally gave up control at that point, happily putting herself in the hands of the friendly ferry crew. She wouldn't take that control back again until she exited the return ferry and landed once more in Hatteras when their week was over. She got out of her car and leaned on the iron rail, watching the ripples of the water passing by and the island of Ocracoke slowly growing larger and closer. Her hair was blowing all around her face; she couldn't stop smiling, but then why should she?

Her stressful job as vice-president of a property management business was a great job in many ways; good pay, good benefits, and long vacations since she'd been there for so many years. And she got to live in the beautiful Outer Banks of North Carolina, a place rich with history from the days of the first European settlers through Blackbeard the Pirate. Later on, the brave Surfmen of the lifesaving stations patrolled the beaches searching for shipwrecks out in the treacherous waters off Cape Hatteras. The keepers of the remote lighthouse stations left many stories to tell as well.

But Sarah's job (like all management positions) was a constant flow of daily stresses that could become almost unbearable at times. Dealing with homeowners, buyers, employees, and then the clients who rented the beautiful vacation homes constantly brought new challenges. It was her job to keep everything running smoothly and keep everybody happy.

Sarah laughed to herself as she remembered the oddball renters. Some people were never happy and would take their frustrations out on her, venting and carrying on like spoiled children. At least it gave her some funny stories to share with her friends every year and they could all have a good laugh over a nice glass of wine about how crazy some of the guests could be!

A few of those tourists would book their vacation on a remote barrier island off the coast of North Carolina, a place known to be subject to floods, hurricanes, unpredictable winds and water – along with everything else that part of the

Atlantic Ocean had to throw at it. And then, if things got even a little dicey, some of them would whine and carry on as if they had reserved a stay at a five-star hotel in Manhattan and expected everything to be just-so... *Oh, well, she wouldn't be dealing with any of them this week!*

She went back to her car and grabbed a soda, taking it back to her spot along the railing. The minute she popped the top and made that *scuusssh* sound, she heard a loud squawking from above; the seagulls had spotted her! Every ferry boat carried along its load of these hitchhikers, sea birds who knew that ferries were great for hunting both the fish that swam around them and the humans who ate food out on the deck. She laughed out loud and dived back into her car to have her soda, frustrating the birds who just *knew* she was in there and that she had some food!

The ferry landed on Ocracoke at last; they unloaded in an orderly fashion and the gaggle of cars all headed south on NC 12 toward the campgrounds and beaches and the tiny village of Ocracoke itself. It was a desolate ride for about twelve miles — just dunes and beach approaches, sea grass, scrubby bushes and trees bent by the constant winds off the ocean. But that short drive, too, was part of the unwinding process and gave Sarah the time to soak up the feel of this beautiful little island.

Suddenly she was there! Sarah inhaled deeply and then exhaled loudly as yet another large smile involuntarily came over her face. The speed limit in the whole town was 20 mph, and there were so many people on bikes and walking around that you'd better do no more than that or you'd take out some unwary, meandering shopper or an unsteady biker who hadn't been on a bike in years until a few days ago. And there was always the chance that you'd encounter some wobbly walker who'd been hanging out at one of the cafes and drinking beer with their lunch!

Sarah was the organizer of the group and always first to arrive; she reserved the cottage and took care of picking up the keys, opening their rented house and getting things ready for the other two, who'd arrive shortly. She opened up all the windows and felt the salty breezes that blew the cotton curtains; this was the prescription she'd needed! As she went about unloading her things, she thought of her two friends who would arrive soon.

Aleta, who lived much closer, always ran a little late. Sarah chalked this up to the fact that artists are easily distracted visually, which causes them to lose track of space and time. But Aleta's happy, laid-back personality more than made up for her little quirks. She was warm, funny, kind and considerate, all qualities that helped Sarah relax whenever they were together. This time Sarah was determined to beat her at *Bananagrams*!

Kate was also a dreamer-type who got caught up in the moment wherever she was, soaking in all the sensual details, which helped her to infuse her settings and characters with the nuances of human feelings and experiences. But Sarah thought of this friend as somewhat of a study in contrasts; Kate was also organized, efficient and thorough, sometimes annoyingly so. But there again, her constant glass-half-full attitude and easy humor made her a pleasure to be around.

Sarah herself had been called a workaholic, but she didn't think of herself that way. She tried hard to be good at her job and had proved over the years that she was invaluable to the company. She was in management, and when you have that kind of job, you just do what you have to in order to get things done. They pay you well, but they expect a lot out of you; it was a trade-off and one she had decided that she could live with.

But her vacations were her salvation; if she could get far enough away, the people at work would think of her as truly *gone* and try to solve their own problems for a change instead of running to her with every little hiccup. Only the worst of situations would make their way to her this week and she could either handle them by phone or delegate them to someone else until she returned.

Sarah, Aleta and Kate always enjoyed being together. These three women friends' personalities and habits were totally complementary; they never fussed over anything and everybody pitched in to get done whatever needed doing. They spent the days doing their own thing and the evenings having fun doing things together, playing games or simply talking.

All of them had husbands but they were the kind of secure, confident men who loved their wives enough to take care of themselves for a week so that their wives could have their important 'girl time.' And that attitude made their wives love and appreciate them all the more when they came back home.

Sarah's planned 'activities' for the week included lots of beach time, reading one or two novels, and taking more than a few naps. Her priority was rest, and she was determined that nothing was going to get in the way of accomplishing her goal. The particular house she'd rented this year looked great in the online photos; it was within sight of the Ocracoke lighthouse, was off to itself and seemed to be perfect for them.

Many of the old island houses had been updated over the years to appeal to a more modern crowd, but still kept their quaint, rustic charm. They had names like 'Sea Biscuit', 'Wisteria Cottage', 'Mattie Midgett Cottage' and 'Fiddler's Rest'. The one she'd chosen this time had looked lovely on the realty's website; it was called 'Sweet Lil's House.' It had a great view of the Ocracoke lighthouse across the marshes from the inviting screened-in back porch, where she planned to spend much of her free time.

So after the other two arrived, hugs were shared all around and they'd unpacked, the women started their first evening by eating a simple meal and opening a bottle of wine. Afterwards, they took their wine in Solo cups and walked to the west side of the island to watch the sun sink lazily into the Sound. They sipped, took photos and visited with other tourists who couldn't get enough of these gorgeous sunsets. Then they strolled back and lit candles for soft lighting on the screened porch and 'assumed their positions' in the wooden porch chairs.

Their first night together usually involved catching up on what had happened to them in the last year: kids, husbands, relatives, friends and news that affected all of them. When that was covered, they moved on to the best part; the *'what do you think?'* and *'what does it mean?'* conversations. And, of course, the *'why do men do that?'* questions that can never be answered by sane women, but are the stuff that ladies find forever intriguing and hysterically funny.

Sarah shared her favorite work story from the past year. A guest who'd rented a huge beach house had called maintenance in the middle of the night with an 'emergency': the ocean was making so much noise that she couldn't sleep – *so what was the company going to do about that and how soon would they get it done?*

The three of them talked and laughed until they couldn't keep their eyes open and eventually admitted that they weren't getting any younger and needed to go to bed.

Sarah smiled as she brushed her teeth, so happy to be back on Ocracoke Island with her friends.

Chapter 3

The next morning Sarah awoke early and decided that a bike ride would be a good way to start her day. She poured on the sunscreen, jumped on the old clunker she'd rented and headed out. The ride around Silver Lake Harbor was beautiful; the morning sun glinted off the small bay, sparkling and moving on the surface like little pieces of glitter that had been tossed haphazardly over the water by some giant hand.

Silver Lake was actually a small natural, protected bay, not more than one-half mile across. The docks and ships settled all around it made it all seem to nestle together in a cozy, inviting way. She paused to take a few photos and made her way into the 'downtown' part of Ocracoke, stopping to get a coffee.

She ended up down by the south landing, the place where the ferries come in and go out to Cedar Island or Swans Quarter. She rode her bike to the nearby boat launch, then walked to the water's edge and out onto the dock over the Pamlico Sound, feeling the wind in her hair and no cell phone in her pocket. She could sense some of the tension melting away from her shoulders; she smiled and laughed out loud. Her hair was being blown all around her face by the wind, she'd left her bra behind and she couldn't care less what she looked like. *Ahhh...freedom!*

As she biked back, Sarah noticed that when you pass people on the street in Ocracoke Village they wave to one another and often say, 'good morning' or 'hey there' (and always give you a big smile). Even if they'd never be brave enough to do something like that back at home, it just seemed to come natural when you were walking or biking down the street in that slow-moving, timeless little village.

When she returned to the cottage, the other two were only just getting up and were drinking tea or coffee out on the porch. She bounded in, smiled at her two bleary-eyed friends and asked who was ready for some breakfast.

"Not yet…" Kate said, yawning and stretching. "Need to wake up first…"

"Maybe later, I'll just grab something," Aleta said, sipping her tea. "What's it like out there today, it looks windy?"

Sarah said, "Oh, it's just the most beautiful morning you could ever wish for! The sun is warm, the wind is cool and the water is sparkling! It's May in Ocracoke!" She waved her hands around and bounced up and down a little.

Kate and Aleta looked at one another and snickered. "I believe that she needed this vacation," Aleta said.

"Ya think?" Kate said, shaking her head. All three of them laughed.

"Okay, if it's that wonderful," Kate said, rising to get dressed, "then I need to get out there and enjoy it before I start writing. I'm a morning person, you know, so one hour's work in the morning is worth two in the afternoon for me."

"That's because you sleep all afternoon, dear," Sarah said. "Hard to get anything done when you're asleep." She grinned.

"Not *all* afternoon!" Kate replied, defensively.

Sarah gave her a look. "You mean to tell us that you're not taking your famous two-hour naps anymore?"

One side of Kate's mouth went up. "Okay, guilty as charged, but they're not always two hours long! Sometimes I only sleep for an hour!"

"And sometimes you sleep for three hours!" Sarah pointed out.

Kate nodded reluctantly but then stuck her chin in the air and tossed her hair back. "Well, yes, it's true. But then, great creative genius requires a lot of rest for the brain!" She laughed out loud. "Right, Aleta?"

"Of course!" Aleta said, nodding. "I just get all mine at night like regular people," she said with a grin.

Kate waved her away. "Oh, ya'll are just jealous that I can sleep so well!"

Sarah smiled and pushed her blonde hair away from her blue eyes. "You're absolutely right! But this time I plan to give you a run for your money when it comes to naps! So, what do ya'll have planned for the day?"

Kate's eyes lit up. "I'm going to work on a new novel that I've just started. This one is about why General Sherman spared a single town when he burned his way through

Georgia on his 'March to the Sea' toward the end of the Civil War. It's called **Saving Madison** and it's going to be a real antebellum adventure!" Her excitement was evident.

"Sounds good, is there going to be love in it? A beautiful heroine and some cad who breaks her heart?" Aleta asked eagerly.

Kate looked offended. "Of course! Plus adventure, politics, the horror of war and the beauty of the human spirit, together with a touch of my usual 'strong person overcomes all odds to find happiness' element. Sound good?"

"You bet!" Sarah said. "Your books help me to relax at night so that I can go to sleep. It's about time you published another one." Turning to Aleta, she said, "And your day?"

Aleta thought for a moment, tilting her head. Her shoulder-length frosted brown hair fell onto her cheek, making Kate think that Aleta's face would make a lovely portrait if only someone would paint *her*.

"I have a commission to do a house portrait, and I also want to do some more scenes around the lighthouse. So when the wind settles down, I'll be outside getting all set up and started on one or the other."

"Well, the morning light is bright and the sky looks clear, so you should have great conditions for your outdoor paintings," Kate said.

"All my paintings are done outside, you know that, Kate," Aleta said, raising one eyebrow. "I'm a plein-air painter," she added, sitting up a little straighter. "We work with nature's gifts of color, value, shadow and light."

Kate rolled her eyes. "Right... *Plein-air*, that's French for working outside getting sunburned, rained on, bug-bit and blown around, isn't it?" She grinned.

"Artists *and* writers are sensitive people who need just the right conditions for their talents to shine, don't we?" Aleta said. She threw a wadded-up napkin at her friend, who laughed and threw it right back at her.

Sarah grinned. "Like the little quiet corners you always find, Kate, where nobody will interrupt your writing with questions or bother you with details about food or anything mundane like that!"

Kate gave her a look. "Hey! I have to create whole worlds in my mind, flesh them out with rich details and then fill them with characters that are appealing, but not *too* likeable, interesting but imperfect, easy to relate to and yet still manage somehow to maintain their individuality, *and then* have them do something that's ordinary but leads to the extraordinary. That's a tad hard to do with people interrupting you all the time with silly little minutia..."

"Spoken with all the adjectives and adverbs of a true writer," Aleta said, making a face at her.

Sarah laughed. "You two are such lovable snobs, but that's why I like being with you, I guess. *I'll* just be hanging out doing nothing, having a vacation, and ya'll go ahead and work your little fingers to the bone. And when I go over to the Jolly Roger to have a beer this afternoon, I won't bother to invite you…"

"Invite me!" Kate said. "Even creative genius needs a break and refreshing libations from time to time!"

"Me, too!" Aleta said eagerly. "All that vigorous outdoor activity makes me dry as a bone when the wind is blowing!"

Sarah laughed and then went inside to begin to prepare her breakfast. She had in mind to bike to the west side of the island where they'd watched the sunset last night, lay in the sun and read for a while. Then she'd come back, have lunch and take a nap, and then either sit in the sun again or just lay around and read some more. Just the kind of *nothing* she'd been dreaming of doing!

"So, where are you going today?" Aleta asked, coming inside, picking up a mango and beginning to peel it.

"I plan to…" Sarah began and then stopped. "Well, let me rephrase that; I'm not *planning* to do anything. I'm going to get on my bike and ride. Then I'll stop. Then I'll lay out in the sun somewhere if I feel like it. Then… I don't know what I'll do." Sarah grinned. "How's that for a plan?"

Aleta smiled. "You're enjoying not having anything to do, aren't you?"

"You bet! So don't ask me my plans, because I'll be making it up as I go along! You're welcome to come with me if you don't care where you're going or when you'll be back..." Sarah shoved the spoon into her bowl of yogurt and granola and stirred.

"Thanks, but this is a working vacation for me, so I'll be out there painting. Then I'll stop when I'm tired and start again when I feel like it, so I suppose we are pretty much on the same schedule, huh?" Aleta said.

"And what about Kate?" Sarah asked.

"Oh, if she's not writing, she'll probably be out riding her bike or in the kitchen organizing everything or labeling something," Aleta said, laughing. "It's the kind of thing she does to relax, you know..."

Sarah shook her head. "To each his own, I suppose! Personally, I want to think as little as possible this week! Give me the sun, a glass of wine and a book, and I'll be happy!"

"Aren't the three of us a sight?" Aleta said. "It's a good thing that we all get along so well and seem to complement one another," she added, looking off into the distance, "like the colors of a sunset."

"Spoken like a true artist," Sarah said with a mouth full of granola. "And like a true friend!"

Chapter 4

When Sarah rolled up to the sandy path that led down to the beach, she got off her bicycle, parked it haphazardly in the rickety old wooden bike rack, unloaded her bike basket and then walked toward the shore. Looking around, she spotted the perfect place to lay out – not too far down but still far enough from everyone else to give her plenty of privacy. She spread out her towel, settled herself in and began to read a new novel.

This particular book was not great, but it wasn't bad, either. She tried to choose books without a lot of gratuitous sex and violence, preferring authors who imbued their stories with believability and characters that could carry the plot without resorting to committing gratuitous violence or rolling around in bed together all the time.

She closed her eyes and listened to the peaceful sound of the water slapping onto the sand; it reminded her of the regularity of a heartbeat, or breathing. Some of the larger waves would hit a little harder than others and make more noise, the more gentle ones softly *splatted* up against the beach. Each wave laid itself down, spent from its journey and then receded into the water to become part of something new.

Sarah loved the ocean. But after a few minutes, she found that just lying or sitting still was not happening for her, so she decided to get up and explore the little area around her. Evidently she was going to have to unwind slowly. She threw on her sandals and walked along the shoreline. On this side of the island, the sandy beaches would slowly dissolve into the sea grass, rushes or perhaps a rocky shoreline that came right out to meet the water. She smiled, enjoying the feel of the sun on her face, the wind over her body and the gentle sound of the water lapping up onto shore.

A little further down, jetties had been built of large rocks. She ambled out a ways on the first one, being careful not to slip on the slick rocks. Looking off toward Portsmouth Island, she emptied her mind and closed her eyes, soaking it all up... until...

A soft noise nearby got her attention. It was irregular and sounded different each time she heard it. First a *ding*, then a *clink*, sometimes with a bit of a *thunk* thrown in there. She opened her eyes and tried to pinpoint the source of the sound, slowly turning her head. Suddenly she caught a flicker of sunlight reflecting off something in the shallow water and rocks in her peripheral vision. Shading her eyes to get a closer look, she stepped a little further down the jetty. Pushing aside the seaweed and debris, she spotted what looked like a glass bottle.

Just somebody who was too lazy to throw their trash in a can, Sarah said to herself. Being a person who loved the planet, she muttered to herself and decided to wade over, fish it out and dispose of it properly when she got back to the cottage. She noticed that it was covered with algae, evidently having floated around for quite some time. She tentatively picked it up with two fingers, expecting it to be filled with brackish water and maybe even have something swimming or crawling in there – but the cork was still in it. It was surprisingly light, but covered in a greenish slime.

She carried it gingerly back to her beach towel and began to scrub sand over it, trying to clean it up a bit and see what, if anything was in it. The label was long gone, but it looked as if someone had corked it and then even covered the cork with melted wax; the thing was sealed up tight! She looked carefully and noticed that there appeared to be some paper rolled up inside.

Could this be what it looked like? If so, she had found an actual message-in-a-bottle! Her heart was pounding with excitement. Was this a love letter or a long-lost call for help? Should she open it? Should she take it to the Ocracoke authorities and turn it over to them? Maybe the historical society would like to have it...

She sat back on her haunches staring at the old bottle and mulling over all her options. Finally she decided to take it back to the cottage and let the three of them figure out together what to do with it. She wrapped the bottle carefully in her big shirt and set it aside. Curiosity was killing her, so she'd have to do something about it soon so that she would be able to focus her mind on her book or anything else! Relaxing with that bottle nearby was going to be hard...

After about a half hour of puttering around by the water, she couldn't stand the uncertainty any longer and decided to head back. She carefully placed the bottle in her bike basket, cushioning it with towels and other soft things. *That's silly of me,* she told herself, *this thing's been rolling around in the water banging against things for a long time, so it must be a sturdy bottle*!

Arriving back at the cottage, she grabbed her prize, bounded up the steps and pushed through the screen door to the back porch, hoping to find the other two still sipping their coffee, but nobody was out there. She went inside and called for them but didn't get an answer. Finally she went from room to room looking for somebody.

Kate was sitting on her bed working on her laptop.

"Didn't you hear me calling you?" Sarah asked, stepping inside the door.

Kate looked up, tilted her head and then raised her left hand to her ear and removed a small spongy pink earplug. "What did you say? I have earplugs in my ears so that I don't get distracted by noise..."

Sarah rolled her eyes. "I was calling both of you! Where's Aleta? I found something amazing!"

"What – what did you find?" Kate said, removing her other earplug.

"All three of us need to be together when I tell you – where is Aleta?"

Kate shook her head and shrugged. "Am I my sister's keeper? She said something about walking down the street a little and painting one of the nearby cottages; didn't you pass her on your way in?"

"No. Maybe she's on the other side of the house. I'll go look for her and in the meantime, you come on out to the porch!"

Kate made a face. "This had better be good, Sarah, I was just getting to an exciting part of the plot and I need continuity of thought to make it realistic. Tell you what – you go find Aleta and then I'll stop what I'm doing, okay?"

Without waiting for an answer, Kate began to finish typing her train of thought and Sarah headed back outside to find Aleta. Sure enough, she had set up her easel a few houses down the street and was seriously involved in painting one of the cute little cottages nearby. She looked up and saw Sarah rushing up. "What?" she asked, startled. "Is everything alright? Is Kate okay?"

Sarah's grin was almost as wide as her face. "I found something amazing – a message in a bottle! You have to come and see!"

Aleta grimaced. "But, Sarah, I just got everything set up and going good; I don't want to have to pack up and drag all this stuff back, then set up again in a few minutes! Tell you what; it can wait until lunch, okay? That'll let me get in a couple of good hours of work..."

Sarah pushed her blonde hair out of her eyes and gave her friend a frustrated look. "But it's a *message in a bottle*, Aleta! Aren't you dying of curiosity? Don't you want to be there when I open it?"

Aleta raised her eyebrows. "Does the bottle look old or new, Sarah?"

"Well, it looks pretty old to me."

"Then it can wait for a couple hours more, don't you think?" Aleta said. "After all these years, what's the rush?"

"Honestly, Aleta, I thought that you'd be all over this!"

"I will be, but I have to work, you know that. You of all people should be able to understand that!"

Sarah exhaled heavily. "Alright, we'll wait till you come back for lunch! But if you're not back by... oh, twelve-thirty, Kate and I are opening it without you!"

"You wouldn't do *that*, would you?" she asked pitifully.

"Oh, alright, we'll wait on you, but don't make us wait long, please?"

Aleta nodded and got back to work. "See you in a couple of hours..."

Back at the cottage, she relayed Aleta's message to Kate, who simply rolled her eyes, put her earplugs back in and went back to her typing, muttering something under her breath about *that cur* General Sherman.

Sarah removed the bottle from the towel and set it on a wooden table out on the porch. Then she took it inside and washed off the last of the gunk. Studying it, she was surprised to see no evidence of mold or mildew on the paper inside, which appeared to be several pages and in fairly good shape.

What could it be? Her thoughts were flitting in all directions. She decided to try to put it out of her mind until lunch, and picked up her not-so-interesting book to read a little more.

Her thoughts were all over the map so she finally put her book down. She decided to Google "message in a bottle" to see what turned up. Evidently there was a book and a movie by that name, but that wasn't what she was looking for. She followed a few more links and discovered that the oldest verified example was a one-hundred-year old message that had been pulled out of the Baltic Sea by a fisherman in April of 2014. It had been written by a twenty year old man and had floated around in the same area for a century after being pitched in!

So it *was* possible that it could be a really old message! She had found it on the west side of Ocracoke Island, so it must have come from somewhere inland, maybe the northern Outer Banks or even the Elizabeth City area. But then, with the way the storms tore through this area on a regular basis, it could have come in on a current in the Atlantic Ocean from just about anywhere!

This bottle didn't appear to be an antique; the green glass was thick and had some numbers and letters stamped on the bottom of it, so it was probably fairly modern. But what in the world did it say? What message could be so important that it would move a person to pour out their thoughts and feelings on paper to be discovered by a perfect stranger at some unknowable future date?

Well, it could be a kid's science experiment, she supposed. After all, didn't every kid who heard about it want to try one? She had been fascinated by the idea as a child but never got around to actually doing it; maybe this kid was more industrious than she had been! But then again, there were several pages in there and usually a kid wouldn't write something that long...

Oh, where were Aleta and Kate! She was dying of curiosity and couldn't wait to open it!

Time dragged by until finally all three of them were together on the porch. Aleta was cleaning her brushes and Kate was sitting in a rocking chair looking off into space, doubtless thinking about her southern heroine or General Sherman. Sarah cleared her throat and started.

"Look, girls, this is really exciting! How can you be so casual about it? It's a genuine message in a bottle!"

"Probably just some kid's project and has a picture they colored or something like that in it..." Kate said, returning to reality.

"What are you gonna do with it?" Aleta asked, concentrating on getting all the paint out of her brushes.

"That's what I need you two for!" Sarah said. "I have to decide what to do with it! Do I take it to the authorities or to the historical society or donate it to a museum?"

Kate laughed. "For Pete's sake, Sarah, just open it! I mean, it's a quaint idea and all, and it'll be fun to read whatever's inside, but I'm sure it's nothing earth-shattering!"

"I agree," Aleta said. "You really don't want to be bothering the police or anybody like that; they'll laugh you right out of there!"

Sarah thought about that. "Okay, so I won't take it to anybody; but should I open it or throw it back into the Sound just like I found it?"

Kate snickered. "Don't you want to know what it says?"

"Of course, I'm dying to know, but somehow it just doesn't feel... right. It would be like invading some stranger's privacy..."

Kate shook her head. "No, Sarah, it wouldn't. If the person who wrote it hadn't wanted anyone to read it, they'd have burned the message instead of putting it in a bottle and throwing it into the sea."

Sarah's face scrunched up. "I suppose you're right about that..."

Aleta put her brushes away finally, wiped her hands and said, "So let's crack it open and see what's in there, everybody agreed?" She sat down, forming a circle with the other two around the bottle lying on the wooden porch table.

Sarah looked at Kate, who nodded. She made up her mind at last. "Okay, but we're not bustin' the bottle; we'll take it apart carefully." The others agreed.

Sarah took a knife and began to carve the wax off the top end of the bottle. "Someone evidently took a lot of care to make this water-tight," she said, scraping away. "This is a pretty thick coating of wax and it goes way down the neck of the bottle. Look!"

Kate and Aleta leaned in. "Wow!" Aleta said. "They *were* careful. What do we do after we get the wax off?

Kate laughed. "You've opened many a bottle of wine in your time, girlfriend, I'm sure that you know how to use a corkscrew!"

"Oh, yes…" Aleta said, smiling. "Some would say that I am an expert in that department."

"Yes, and you're my *favorite* wine snob," Kate said to her, poking her in the arm.

"But then anybody who doesn't share your cultivated taste in *box wines* is a wine snob, Kate!" she said, poking her back. It was an old standing joke between them that they'd played around with for years. Both of them shared a big smile.

"Yes, I have a definite preference for box wines, or 'Cardboardeaux' as I have come to call it," Kate said.

Sarah laughed so hard that she snorted. "Back to business here," she said, "somebody go get the corkscrew, we're ready for that part."

Aleta did the honors and the cork came out smoothly. "It doesn't smell as bad as I thought it would," she said, sniffing the bottle and passing it around for the others to do the same.

"I just assumed it would have a musty smell to it," Kate said.

"It must have been airtight all these year, between the cork and all that wax," Sarah said. "Now we need to get the message out…" She took the bottle, turned it upside down, shook it, and the tightly wound papers scooted toward the top. They looked to be bound with a rubber band, probably so that the sender could get all of the paper in through the neck of the bottle. Sarah gave it another little shake and the wad inched closer to the end. Finally she was able to get hold of it with a pair of tweezers and pulled it out slowly.

The old rubber band fell apart almost immediately, causing the tube of papers to relax and open up a little. Sarah touched them gently. They didn't seem terribly fragile, but she could tell that they were old, written on what looked like pieces of lined tablet paper. The writing on the outside yellowed pages looked faded but the pages themselves felt fairly sturdy.

"So? What does it say? Tell us!" Kate said, rubbing her hands together.

Sarah carefully unrolled the tight tube of papers, noticed the large scrawling hand it was written in, and began to read aloud:

"Ocracoke Island, NC,

November, 1981

I'm putting these words on paper and into a bottle because, well, it looks like I'll be gone before too much longer and I don't want to die with this heavy burden on my heart. It's been my load to carry for all these years and I have got to lay it down before I go to meet my Maker.

My name is Virgil Timmons and I am one of the ones who did what came to be called the Buffalo City Moonshine Murders. Well, I didn't kill them girls or get rid of their bodies, but the whole thing was partly my fault too, when you come right down to it. At least I've come to think of it like that because I might could have stopped it if I'd tried harder.

You see, back in '32, I was just a kid, only 18 yrs old. Now I'm an old man and if I knew then what I know now, I'd sure have told the truth rather than keep quiet about the whole thing, which is what I did back then.

Because I was just a scared kid who didn't know what to do and my friend Sasha, well, I let him talk me into it and I shouldn't have let him do that because it was wrong. But he was one big, mean Russian and you didn't argue with Sasha nor Ryan neither and live to tell about it.

I never even told my wife Lillian about what happened that day. As far as I know, only one man besides the three of us ever knew that I was involved in that terrible affair, and he never told nobody. That was Lucky O'Rourke from up around Norfolk, and a finer man you'd never meet if you lived a hundred years. He understood what it was like for me and he kept my secret. I went to his funeral when he died and didn't talk to nobody there. I just went and watched them lower that box into the ground – him and my secret together with him.

But even after Lucky died, the guilt didn't go away like I thought it might. It's been stuck in my craw ever since it happened, and before I die I have to admit to it the world.

I pretty much growed up in Buffalo City, cause I was either born there or we moved there when I was just a little bit of a thing and I don't remember anything before that. My Pa was a foreman at the lumber mill and we lived in one of the nicer red houses in town. We wasn't rich or nothing like that, but we had a little money, especially compared to some of the Russians and black folks that they brought in to work there. We always had clothes and shoes and food, and back in them days that was considered pretty well-off.

But then my Pa got killed in that accident at the mill and me and my Ma stayed there in Buffalo City because we really didn't have no place else to go. Life was hard for us, me and Ma. And she made it even harder by being so mean all the time. She was a mean woman, my Ma, right down til the day she died. But that's another story.

Buffalo City was a lumber town, and in its hay-day back in the early 1900's, it was the biggest settlement in the whole of Dare County, what with it having about 3,000 people living there. Nowadays there ain't much left out there in the woods, just a few rails and a foundation or two.

Back when the lumber trade was going good, Buffalo City was a right nice place to live. We were out in the swampy lowcountry of North Carolina it's true, and a long way from any big towns, but back then everything was a long way from everything else and there wasn't no quick way to get nowhere. You took a wagon or a boat, or you took a rail car if there was one running, or you stayed put right where you was.

Nowadays there's some nice big bridges to take you out there and tourists pay good money to go out to the beaches over around Cape Hatteras and such, but back then that part of the Outer Banks was just a bunch of sandy dunes that got blowed around by the wind and washed away during the hurricanes and nobody except a few life-saver men or fishermen much thought it would ever be a decent place to live.

The storms that blow up there can be evil sometimes to the point where a person thinks they're not going to survive. There's a ton of shipwrecks out off those islands and most of them ain't even been found yet. They're down in the devil's hold, the bottom of the hungry sea.

But what I want to tell has nothing to do with the beaches, it's about what happened in 1932 on the Pasquotank River somewhere near Elizabeth City. I'm not sure exactly where we was when it took place... all I remember is that it happened real fast...

All these years I've been telling myself that I didn't have nothing to confess, but that's not the truth. Not really. I was involved in the illegal liquor trade and that alone was breaking the law. I made me some good money hauling moonshine, too, and I spent my ill-gotten gains without remorse building a nice little house for my sweet wife.

But after I married Lillian, I tried to be a good person and never did nothing illegal again, that is if you don't count an occasional poker game and such. And I even went to church once in a while, though it didn't seem to make a lot of sense to me that a god of love would torture people for all eternity for just making a mistake or two in their lives. But then the preacher told me that understanding all of that was too hard for somebody as simple as me, and he was probably right.

So, what I need to confess is this: even though I didn't kill those two girls (they were sisters, it turned out) or get rid of their bodies, I was in on it, and that's what I want to admit. I was there, but I wasn't part of the actual killing. But that makes me what I found out they call an accomplice.

I reckon that God will have to figure out what he's gonna do to me for that, and I also reckon that I'll be taking whatever punishment He dishes out to me because I deserve it. But I tell you this, it couldn't be much worse than what my conscience has been doing to me for almost fifty years now.

So, whoever finds this message, whenever it is, I ask you to tell whoever you think needs to know that I was in on those murders. That is, if you feel like it's the right thing to do. But I beg you, please don't drag my family into it because none of them never knowed nothing about it.

I was there and I was part of it. You can believe me or not believe me, I reckon, as to whether I'm innocent or guilty.

And whatever you decide to do with this information you can work it out with God between you and Him. If you're the kind of person who's made some mistakes too, and I'm in a position to put in a good word for you with Him, I will.

Thank you,

Virgil Timmons"

"Is that all it says?" Kate asked, wide-eyed.

Sarah shuffled the pages around, looking carefully on the back of each one. She glanced up at the other two, who were leaning forward in their chairs and hanging on her every word.

"It must be," she said, stacking the papers back together. "A man named Virgil Timmons wanted to confess to being part of something he called 'the Buffalo City moonshine murders' that involved two girls who were sisters. Either of you ever heard of anything like that?"

Both the other women shook their head. "I never heard of Buffalo City – where in the world is that?" Kate asked.

Aleta said, "I believe that it's somewhere over west of Manteo and Manns Harbor – or at least it used to be. It's a ghost town now, or not even that really. We took a guided kayak trip out there a few years back and there's no sign that there was ever a town there, except maybe a piece of rail where the train ran..."

The three of them stared blankly at one another.

"I'll Google 'Buffalo City' and let's see what turns up," Sarah said, reaching for her ipad. "Hmmm... look here, some pictures came up and it does look like it was a logging town..." She passed the pad around to the others, who studied the photos as she said, "Well, I'm going to do some more research on this and find out about these 'moonshine murders' that supposedly happened there. Do you think this is real or some kind of a joke?" she asked, pointing to the papers.

Kate said, "Why would somebody make up something like that? It's too real, too detailed to be made up. And the wine bottle, the paper – it's obviously old. When did it say he wrote it?"

Sarah looked at the first page. "It says, '1981' and it was written here in Ocracoke." She looked at her friends. "It has all the markings of the truth – an actual date and place and event...

Kate nodded. "So, it seems to fit the facts as far as I can tell... it's probably not a joke."

Sarah sat up straight. "Alright then, I'm going to investigate the whole thing and see what I can turn up. You two have stuff to do, so I'll be in charge of this and whatever I find out I'll share with you."

"Well, we can discuss it in the evenings, but I do need to get back to work..." Aleta said, standing up. "Just as soon as I get some lunch, that is."

"And a nap, too!" Sarah said, grinning at her friend. "We can't forget that!"

Kate laughed out loud and nodded. "Definitely a nap!"

Sarah spent the next hour or so researching Buffalo City. It was just like Virgil and Aleta had said, once a boom town and now a ghost town which the swampy lowlands had reabsorbed to the point that the area looked as if the town had never existed.

When she searched 'Buffalo City Moonshine', all that turned up was a few more articles about the town and how they had indeed made some of the best moonshine ever to be had. Turned out that a few people remained who had lived there then, and a local Outer Banks author named Suzanne Tate had interviewed them and recorded their memories in a book called "Logs and Moonshine."

Sarah went to amazon.com to download the ebook and found that the only copies were print copies. She needed that book *now* and couldn't wait for a delivery. So jumping on her bike, she headed over to talk to Leslie at the local bookshop, *Books To Be Red*. Together, they looked through the local history books for sale, but nothing else on Buffalo City could be found.

Leslie did have a copy of *Logs and Moonshine*, so Sarah scooped that up. Not wanting to pry, Leslie didn't ask why Sarah was looking for the information, but she tried to help her and also recommended that she head over to the Ocracoke Preservation Museum down by the ferry dock. Sarah thanked Leslie for her help and made a note to herself to come back. *Books To Be Red* was not only a bookstore, but a lovely eclectic gift shop as well and she had some gifts to buy. This would be the perfect place.

The Museum, built in an old house, was a place that she could get lost in (and had several times). The last time she'd been there she had studied the storm stories and then watched a delightful short film on the strange words and terms that the people of Ocracoke had developed as their own unique expressions, the 'Ocracoke Brogue.'

She asked Amy, the museum administrator, if she'd ever heard of a man named Virgil Timmons. The kind and friendly woman looked up and thought for a long moment. "No, I can't say that I have. Perhaps one of the volunteers knows of him and could give you some information... Come back another day if you can."

Sarah pumped Amy for more details about Ocracoke in the 1930's and then left. Now more intrigued than ever, she went back to the house and devoured the short book, *Logs and Moonshine*. Getting a feel for Buffalo City, she could almost visualize the railroad track running down the middle of the main road through the place, with red houses on one side and white houses on the other. The old photos showed a town not unlike photos of the old west. Nothing about any murders was mentioned.

What could possibly have happened all those years ago? Who was this Virgil Timmons, really? Had he committed murder or was he, like he claimed, just an innocent bystander? It sounded like a terrible crime! Sarah leaned her head back and closed her eyes to think about it.

Chapter 5

Virgil's Story

****

Buffalo City
Dare County, North Carolina
May, 1931

The strapping young Russian man paddled his old canoe along the banks of the Alligator River slowly, all the while looking around from side to side for smoke from a fire or that certain particular yeasty smell. Sasha had mapped out the course he'd taken so far from creek to creek, trying to find the moonshiner named Russell and his still that he'd heard about. He wanted to get in on the action and make some real money.

Suddenly he heard a shot in the distance and somebody hollering. He dragged his paddle, stopped still and listened. Out in these woods, the moonshiners were everywhere and didn't take kindly to strangers poking around, so he needed to be careful. But his curiosity got the better of him, so he leaned in and stroked harder, pushing his canoe in the direction of where he guessed the sound of the shot had come from.

He heard more yelling and then a second shot. Determining its direction more accurately, he paddled that way and then glided toward the riverbank, hauling the canoe up onto land as quickly and quietly as possible. Then Sasha heard more hollering and what sounded like somebody running through the woods. He hunkered down behind a big bush, trying to become less of a target and not get himself openly involved in the melee.

A scruffy-looking man came running in his general direction, limping, holding his right thigh, and looking back over his shoulder. Sasha couldn't be sure, but he didn't think he recognized this man. They were miles from Buffalo City and a long way from any other settlement as far as he knew.

"Stop right there, you dirty thief!" he heard yelled from behind the man. "Stop or I'll kill you with the next shot!"

The limping man slowed down and then bent over, grabbing his knees and gasping for breath. He looked as though he was so weak he could barely stand; he turned slowly to face the man chasing him.

His pursuer came running into the clearing, pointing a gun at the runner and stopping about twenty feet away from him. Better dressed and older, the man with the gun clearly held the upper hand. "I got you now, you dirty, lowdown, good-for-nuthin! I give you a job and then what do you do? You try to *steal* from me, will you?"

"It weren't stealin', I was just... rearranging some of your 'quipment! I was gonna... put it back!" the injured man sputtered.

"You're a pitiful thief and a worse liar, Turner! You was gonna put it on the dingy and take off with it! I told you I'd pay you when we found some of the moonshiners in these parts and git set up with 'em hauling their stuff, but you couldn't wait, you had to steal from me! I'm gonna tie you up and take you back to Wilmington and let the law deal with the likes of you!"

"Alright, I give up!" the man shouted, holding up his left hand while his right hand kept the blood flow down to a minimum on his thigh. He appeared to be badly injured. "I give up, I said!" he spouted, breathing heavily.

Closing in on his prey, the man with the gun approached slowly. "You're hurt bad, so don't give me no grief or I'll finish you off right here and now, you understand?"

Sasha gasped and ducked further behind the bush.

"Yessir, Mr. Hillburn," the man said, grimacing with pain. "I understand."

"Lay down on your belly and put your hands behind your back now," he said to his prisoner, waving the gun around.

"But my leg's bleedin' bad, I got to keep a hold on it!" he said. "I'll bleed out right here 'iffin I don't!"

The man with the gun thought it over. "Alright, then, just stay there and do what I tell you. Take off that rope you're wearin' to hold up your britches and tie off your leg to slow the bleedin, and then we'll see what to do."

Turner nodded and began to remove the rope slowly from his raggedy trousers. The man with the gun stood back and watched. Suddenly the injured man fell backwards, collapsing onto the earth as if dead.

"Lord, no, don't let him be dead!" the pursuer said, rushing forward. He tucked the gun into the back of his pants and started to lean over to check the man for signs of life. Just as his hand touched the man's throat, he felt his feet kicked out from under him. "Whatinuh?" he yelped, falling forward.

The injured man took advantage of his pursuer's downward momentum and met his jaw with a roundhouse punch that knocked Hillburn out cold. He fell limply on top of Turner, the man on the ground, who promptly pushed him over and off. He looked around for the gun, spotted it in the back of Hillburn's pants, grabbed it and stood up. Apparently his thigh injury, while definitely bleeding, had not been as bad as he'd made it out to be.

Sasha squatted, peeking out from behind the bush, to see what would happen next, his eyes wide and his heart racing.

Looking down at the unconscious man, Turner laughed. "You didn't know who you were messin' with, did you, *Boss*?" he said, nudging the limp body with his foot. The man stirred and moaned, coming around slowly.

Hatred seethed from Turner's filthy face. "Thought you'd take me in to the law-man, huh? Not while there's breath in this body, you won't! I took the job with you 'cause I was runnin' from the law already and needed to get away from Wilmington. You needed somebody to help you haul illegal liquor and I was ready to go! But you been wanderin' around here long enough, I'm tired of your promises! I was only stealin' from a rumrunner – huh! – so that ain't stealin' at all!"

The man on the ground moaned and opened his eyes. When he focused on the gun pointed at him he said, "Don't shoot me, Turner! I won't turn you in, I promise!" He held out his hands in front of his face and shook his head. "Let's go back to the boat and I'll see about your leg! Just don't shoot me!"

Turner laughed and moved around nervously, shifting the gun from hand to hand. His voice took on a hysterical note as he said, "Shoe's on the other foot now, ain't it, Bossman? Don't worry, I won't steal nuthin off that boat of yours cause it's *my boat* now! You ain't nuthin but a bootlegger and nobody's gonna miss your ugly face! 'Specially me!"

He leaned forward, shot the man in the chest twice and then fired once more. Hillburn twitched and then went totally limp.

Sasha flinched, drew back and almost fell over, just managing to keep his balance.

Turner kicked the body for good measure. "Mess with me, will ya? See where that got ya? Now I got your boat and you ain't got nuthin!" He spat on the body. He looked all around cautiously, decided that nobody had seen or heard anything and headed off through the woods.

Sasha had just witnessed cold-blooded murder and knew that whatever happened from here on out, his own life was now taking a turn. He followed Turner from behind, as quietly as possible. The man limped through the woods a short distance until he came to a little feeder creek, one Sasha had yet to explore on this trip. The injured man headed for a boat anchored close to the creek bank, waded out and with great difficulty hauled himself up the rope ladder and onto the deck, where he collapsed onto a seat on the side of the boat.

The young Russian man sat in the woods and thought about what he'd just witnessed – and what it could mean for him. He sat quietly for over an hour; evidently Turner was too injured or weak to operate the boat yet because he heard no sounds of life up there. Sasha turned back and headed for his canoe. Using his keen insight of these backwaters, he navigated out and around until he located that particular creek and paddled up to the boat. Standing up in the canoe, he shouted, "Hey there, anybody aboard?"

He heard a moan and then Turner lifted his head up, looking around until he spotted him. "What you want?" he shouted. "I got a gun, git away from me!"

"Alright, I vill be going now," Sasha said, holding up his palms and sitting down in the canoe. He grabbed the paddle and looked at Turner, who was glaring down at him. "Do you need some help, meester? You don't look too good..."

Turner managed to get himself up on one leg and then stared at Sasha for a long moment. "You know anything about tendin' to gunshot wounds, boy? I done shot myself, uh... by accident... and I'm bleedin' here. It ain't too bad, but it's hurtin' like hot fire! If you can help me, I'd appreciate it, that I would."

"I'll be right over!" Sasha said, paddling hard toward the larger boat, and then jumping into the water. Climbing the rope ladder, he eased himself up and over the rail slowly. "I am Sasha, from Buffalo City, and I have taken care of gunshot vounds before. First thing ve got to do is stop this bleeding," he said, easing his way over toward the man who was still holding the gun. "And you can put that gun down now, you have already shot yourself and you don't need to be shooting me," he said in a soothing voice, adding a small laugh. "Ve don't vant two accidents here."

Turner seemed to relax a little and stuck the gun into the front of his pants, which were now hanging on him because he'd lost his rope belt in the woods. "Grab that rope over there and tie off my leg," he said to Sasha, pointing to a short piece on the deck.

Sasha lost no time in doing his best to stop the bleeding. After tying the tourniquet, he looked around for some rags and fashioned a bandage. "Looks like the bullet vent clean through the meat, Meester, so if ve can stop the bleeding, you be okay," he said. "Vhat's your name and vhere you are from?" he asked, sitting back on his heels now that the medical work was done.

Turner adjusted his position to elevate the injured leg a bit. "Name's, uh... *Hillburn* and this here's my boat," he said, eyeing Sasha to see how the lie was going over.

"Good to meet you, Mr. Hillburn, like I said, my name is Sasha Sidorov and I'm from Buffalo City, up the river a good long vay," he said, motioning with his chin in a general direction toward the north. "Vhat can I do for you now? Do you need help running your boat? You look like you could use a hand..."

Turner focused his bleary eyes on the young man. "You sound like some kinda fur'ner or somethin'! How would you know how to handle a boat like this?" he asked skeptically.

Sasha nodded. "Da, my folks from Russia, but I was born here in this country and I been raised around boats." He stood up cautiously and walked over to the wheelhouse, poked his head inside and looked around. "This boat be no problem, Mr. – uh... – Hillburn. Let me tie up my canoe to the back and then I take you... vhere you vant me to take you?" He turned to the injured man, extending his hands in a questioning manner.

"To where the nearest doctor can be found, I reckon, boy. Where's that?"

"Ve got us a sort-of doctor in Buffalo City. It's some miles away, but in a boat like this one ve can maybe get there before the dark sets in if ve take off now. Does that sound good?"

Turner nodded, relaxing back against the side of the boat. "Alright. Do it and let's git goin'. I need to see a doc and get this leg sewed up and the bleedin' stopped." He watched as Sasha quickly dropped down the rope ladder, tied his little canoe to the back of the boat and then re-boarded and started up the engine.

"There's moonshiners in these voods, Mr. Hillburn, so ve need to get out of here and out on the river where nobody'll bother us. Ve don't need to make these men angry 'cause they are a hard bunch." Turner nodded and Sasha backed the boat out to deeper water, watching as Turner's head lolled back against the side of the boat. Evidently the blood loss was taking its toll and the man had passed out.

Sasha navigated his way back out to the river and headed toward Mill Tail Creek and home. Turner was out for at least an hour, but then finally came around and croaked, "Water! I need some water!"

Sasha stopped the boat, got a bucket and a dipper and brought the man water. Turner guzzled it down and then his eyes cleared. He squinted at Sasha as if to remember who he was.

"It's me, Mr. Hillburn, Sasha," he said, helping the man sit up straight. "You shot yourself and I came along and helped you out, remember?"

Turner looked confused at first but then nodded slowly. "Yeah. Thanks, boy, I owe you for that."

And you'll be paying me, too, for a long, long time, Sasha thought as he went back to the wheelhouse. They chugged on up Mill Tail Creek toward Buffalo City. Sasha's quick mind was calculating all the ways that this arrangement could work nicely out for him. He'd just hired on to help a man whose nastiest secret he knew.

As they cruised up the wide, winding creek, Sasha tried to plan out the best way to handle this situation; he'd force the man to take him on as a partner. But he realized that if he pushed this fellow too hard, he could easily become the next victim. He grinned at the thought that he was in with a man who owned a boat now and could make big money running moonshine; Sasha wouldn't have to settle for a few dollars working for somebody else...

So if he handled it right, his constant need for money would soon be over. Sasha smiled, feeling better than he had in a long time, despite having been a witness to murder. His future was looking up.

As Sasha was drawing closer to Buffalo City he began having second thoughts about all his plans. Turner was a mean, desperate man and had been pushing him hard despite the fact that Sasha had more or less rescued him. Being in business with him wouldn't be easy and he would never be able to turn his back on the man.

Before reaching the settlement, Sasha decided to get some reinforcements. Turner had fallen asleep again, so Sasha cruised on past Buffalo City, moving further into the woods. He slowly brought the boat towards land and came to a stop, dropping anchor near the creek bank. At that point, Turner woke up, came limping around and hollered, "What you doin? Why we stoppin? We there yet?"

"No, Mr. Hillburn, I just need to get some help. I can't git you off the boat all by myself. My friend Ryan lives here and he'll come vid us and help me get you onto my canoe and onshore."

"What we need help for? Cain't we just pull up to a dock?" Turner spat at him angrily.

"No, sir, ve cannot. The docks are for the boats that come in to the sawmill. Buffalo City is a logging town and the loggers and fishermen are the ones who get the docks. Ryan can help us," he answered, glaring back at the man. "He's just one fellow, like me but not Russian."

Turner appeared to think it over, not noticing Sasha's convoluted logic or flimsy excuses. He could feel himself getting weaker, so he reluctantly nodded his head in agreement. "Make it fast, Russian!" he muttered, and collapsed back onto the deck in obvious pain.

Sasha secured the boat in deeper water and then left on his canoe, stepping out into knee deep water to pull it ashore. He walked back to the shack where Ryan and his family lived. Ryan had been out of work like himself, so he expected to find him home; sure enough he was out in the yard chopping wood.

Sasha whistled, got Ryan's attention and motioned him over to the trees where he was standing.

The other young man glanced up, caught sight of Sasha and walked over. "Whatcha hidin' out in the woods for, Sasha?" Ryan asked, looking around. "You runnin' from somethin' or somebody?" A big grin passed his face. "Some girl's daddy, maybe?"

Sasha grabbed his arm and pulled him over into the bushes so that they would not be visible from the house. Ryan jerked his arm back testily and growled, "What's this about?"

"Vell, it is a long story, but I vill try to make it as short as possible," Sasha began, and then proceeded to tell him all about what had happened down the river earlier in the day, as well as what the current situation was like out on the boat.

Ryan listened to the whole story but then looked at Sasha as if he had grown a third eye. "You're helpin' a murderer? You want me to go out on that boat and help him, too? Just how stupid do you think I am? I know we're friends and all, but I ain't about to go out there and help some murderin' thief" – he stopped suddenly and squinted at Sasha. "Not unless there's somethin' in it for me!"

Sasha laid his big hand on his much shorter friend's shoulder. "Not to help him, Ryan, but to help ourselves to make a lot of money! Ve make him share his profits from hauling moonshine vith us and ve be much better off, don't you see? I can hold it over his head that I know about him killing the man who owned the boat and he'll have to cut us in on the money he makes!"

Ryan backed up, causing Sasha's hand to drop. "So we'll either git rich or he'll kill us in our sleep and throw our bodies into the Sound, you mean! No, Sasha, I ain't gittin involved in that, no way, no how!" He shook his head, held up his hands palms forward and took another step back.

"But he's too sick to hurt us, he cannot even stand himself up!" Sasha said, running his large hand back through his thick blond hair.

Ryan raised an eyebrow, crossed his arms and said nothing for over a minute. Then he stepped forward and put his hand on Sasha's shoulder. "Just how bad off is he, exactly?"

Sasha shook his head. "He von't die, but he has lost a lot of blood. I think if ve get him to the doctor he vill live and all..."

Ryan got a strange look on his face and then nodded. "Just lemme go to the house and tell Ma I'll be gone for a while, and I'll be right back," he said, then turned and trotted back toward the house.

Sasha tilted his head and wondered at Ryan's sudden change of mind, but then shrugged and folded his arms, leaning against a nearby tree. Ryan was a strange bird sometimes; Sasha was often surprised by his behavior, but Ryan never did anything for nothing. The important thing was that he now had the help he needed.

When the two young men returned to the boat, Turner was asleep on a tarp on deck. Sasha shook him gently. "Mr. Hillburn, vake up, I got us some help!"

Turner came around, spotted the two of them and said, "Git off my boat, I don't need no help!" He tried to pull himself up, heading toward the wheelhouse.

Ryan and Sasha walked around in front of him. Sasha said, "Mr. Hillburn, ve are only going to get you to the doctor…"

Turner glared at them, his feverish eyes filling with hatred. "No, you're gonna kill me and steal my boat – I know what you're gonna do!" He crawled toward where the gun lay on the deck.

Ryan rushed over and picked up the gun. Turner stopped crawling and collapsed, losing consciousness again.

Sasha ran over to him and felt for a heartbeat. "He's only passed out, but ve got to get him to the doctor, Ryan!" he said, standing and heading toward the wheelhouse.

"Sasha, wait just a minute," Ryan said in a low voice.

Sasha turned, and stared at Ryan, who still had the gun in his hand, pointing at the back of Turner's head. "Vhat are you doing, Ryan?" he yelled, rushing back to him. "Vhat are you thinking of doing? You're not going to kill him, are you?"

The side of Ryan's mouth lifted slightly. "Ain't nothin but what he deserves! He's a cold-blooded murderer! We can just save the lawman a hangin' and do the job ourselves!"

"I have never killed anything that I did not eat, and for sure not a person!"

Ryan stared at him. "I have. I've put down all kinds of lame animals, bothersome critters and even shot a bunch just for fun. It's not hard. Besides," he added, kicking Turner's still body, "this'un deserves it, you know he does!"

"But ve need him and his boat, Ryan! Ve now can make some real money!"

Ryan thought about it. "We need the *boat*, Sasha, that's for sure, but I don't see as how we need this good-for-nuthin to go with it; besides, it ain't even really his boat! You and me, we can keep the boat for ourselves and do just fine – we wouldn't have to give him nuthin'; we could keep his part if we got rid of him!"

Sasha froze in his tracks. Killing Turner had not even occurred to him. But Ryan was right – if they got rid of him, the boat would be all theirs. And they wouldn't have to put up with the man, either, or worry that he might sneak up and kill them at any time.

"Let's just throw him overboard, then."

Ryan shook his head. "He might live. He might come around and come after us... No, we gotta kill him.!"

"I am not sure I can do it," Sasha said simply, thinking it over.

Ryan looked back toward his house. "Then you can watch me do it! Take us out in the deep water right now!" He turned and grabbed the rope to the anchor and began to pull it up. Turner lay unconscious where he had fallen. "Get us moving, Sasha!"

"But..." the Russian began weakly. The thought of all that money and having his own boat was beginning to take hold in his mind, however, and soon Sasha found himself walking back and starting up the boat's engine.

They got out to deep water and Turner began to stir. Sasha stopped the boat and looked at Ryan. "If you shoot him, they vill hear the shot in town from this close and somebody vill come out looking..." he said, shaking his head.

Ryan nodded. "You're right." He thought about it and quickly came to a decision. "I'll smother him instead. He's weak with pain and there's not a lot of fight left in him, it won't be hard at all and it'll be over quick like that," he said, snapping his fingers. He reached for some dirty rags that lay against the wheelhouse. "You hold him down."

Sasha stepped tentatively toward Turner, who was coming around and beginning to make some noise. "Git off my boat! I'll kill you!" the wounded man muttered, trying his best to sound threatening.

Ryan looked at Sasha. "You see? He would've killed us, you know he would. He might use us for a little while before he got rid of us, but a man like him wouldn't feel bad at all about it, except maybe for the loss of a bullet!"

"No!" Turner squeaked, now aware enough to size up the situation. "I will share with you! I will give ya'll part of the boat!" He began to struggle to sit up.

"You see, Sasha, you see the kind of man he is? I'm gittin this over with!" Ryan grabbed the rags, balled them up and stuffed them against the man's mouth and nose as he sat on Turner's legs. Sasha reluctantly bent over and held down the weak but flailing arms. He watched as the life slowly left the man's skinny body and finally Turner went limp. Sasha stood up, backing away, only to find himself up against the rail. He felt dizzy, turned and threw up over the side of the boat, gagging until he thought that he'd turned his insides out.

He turned to look at Ryan, who was calmly studying the body. A sly smile crossed Ryan's face. He stood up, dusted off his hands on his pants and said, "It wasn't really murder, you know. He might'a died anyway, he was that bad off. We just cut it a little short, that's all – probably even saved the fool some sufferin'. Well, now we only got to get rid of the body. We could either take him off deep in the woods for the animals to eat or we could sink him down to the bottom of the river. Whatcha think? Which would be better?"

Sasha swallowed hard and would have thrown up again if there had been anything at all left in his stomach. Ryan had asked him that question in the same tone of voice that he'd used many times before to ask him, "Ya wanna go huntin' today or maybe play some cards?" The sudden realization of what they had done – and he had helped by holding Turner down – hit Sasha hard. But this was no time to have regrets, it was all done. Now they had to deal with it. He stood up straight.

"Sink him to the bottom," Sasha said. "If ve leave him out in the voods around here, somebody'll find his body." He looked up at Ryan. "But ve better cut him up some, I think. That way the gators'll eat him up that much faster."

Ryan shook his head. "Naw, on second thought, that won't work. Bodies git full of gas after awhile and come floatin' up, and the whole thing or some pieces could wash up on shore... That would cause a big stink and somebody might connect it with us gittin' ourselves a boat..." Ryan waved his hand and dismissed the suggestion.

Sasha thought hard and wondered how Ryan would know that much about dead bodies. "Vhy don't ve take him back to vhere the first man was and bury them both? If somebody stumbled across that first body, they vould start investigation; but if ve bury both of the bodies, then nobody ever figure out vhat happened to either one of them!

Ryan made a face of agreement, nodded, and that was that. "Good thinkin', Sasha!"

They cruised slowly back past Buffalo City as it was beginning to get dark. They pulled over to the creek bank and dropped anchor and slept on the boat. The next morning the boys headed back down the Alligator River and eventually found the spot where the murder had occurred. They stripped both bodies of anything valuable and then threw them into a shallow grave. They filled it with dirt and covered the site with pine needles and leaves.

Sasha was feeling better and better about the whole thing as time was passing. He was now a boat owner! The feeling of power that came over him made his head swim a little; he'd been in on murder and – except for his weakness at first – he was not even sorry for anything; in fact, truth be told, it made him feel like a man to be reckoned with. They headed back to the boat and got aboard.

The two of them looked at one another and smiled. A lot had happened, but the end of it all was that, murder aside, they now had possession of a boat called the *Wilmington Woman* and could go into business for themselves.

"C'mon, Sasha, let's celebrate!" Ryan said, carrying over a jug of 'shine he'd found onboard. "We got ourselves a boat!"

"And ve are going to be rich and powerful!" the big blonde Russian proclaimed, pounding his chest. "Ve vill be big men in Buffalo City!"

Chapter 6

"Ma, I ain't gonna be out late, so just git off my back about it!" Virgil said, waving his arms and then grabbing the door handle to leave the hot, cramped kitchen.

His mother made a face, pointed at the floor and yelled, "Git your tail back in here right now, boy!"

The tall young man stopped, hung his head and then slowly turned around, glaring but saying nothing. Virgil sized her up. Her graying hair was pulled so back tightly into a bun that her eyebrows were a little higher than usual – he figured that fact alone could probably put her in a bad mood. And while his mother was not a fat woman, she was tall, broad, as strong as an ox and could beat him stupid any day of the week. He was only seventeen and thin; and besides all that it *just wasn't right* to hit your mamma.

"I told you that you ain't goin'! So you ain't goin!" his mother said, with her teeth clamped together and only her lips moving. A few renegade strands of sweat-soaked hair hung around her face. She squinted at him, put her fists on her hips and stood there, just hoping for some backtalk from the boy so that then she could give him another good thrashing. Thrashing the boy somehow made her feel a bit better about her miserable life...

He sighed heavily and flopped down into an old straight chair at the table, holding up one hand in a pleading motion. "Ma, I never ask to go *nowhere*, and you know that's the truth! I only want to go down to the docks and hang around with Sasha and Ryan. We won't git in no trouble, I swear!"

She snorted. "That Russian and the Irish scum he hangs around with ain't nuthin but bad news, you hear me? I done told you to stop spending time with 'em! And you ain't goin' nowhere till you git on out there and chop up the rest of that firewood and bring in enough for me to cook breakfast in the mornin'! And I want some of them little pieces, too, for kindlin', you hear me?" She glared at him.

He glanced over at the wood box beside the cook stove. The thing was half-full, and it was warm weather besides. Then he looked up at her. *It must be something else bothering her*, he figured, because she was just being spiteful and didn't want him to go out and have any fun at all.

He exhaled loudly. "Yes, Ma'am," he said, figuring that the course of least resistance was simply to do what she said and then high-tail it out of there quick-like before she realized that he had gone. He stood up, moved toward the back door and then went out, careful not to slam it behind him.

She caught the door just before it closed and leaned out. "Chop it **all** up, now, you hear me?" she hollered after him.

"Yes'sum," he muttered, moving toward the big pile.

"Uh-huh! You *had better* say 'yes, Ma'am' when you talk to me, boy!" she said, slamming the door and getting the last word as always. She mumbled something else as she walked back into the kitchen, but Virgil tried not to hear whatever that might have been. Even if he hadn't done anything, it seemed like he was always in trouble with her for one thing or another!

As he chipped away at the pile, Virgil remembered a time when his mother was not nearly so mean; it had been back before his daddy was killed in that mill accident five years ago. In those days she used to be almost nice sometimes. She even laughed a little. But no more! Now she was all business and as mean as a wounded bear! She never had any fun and didn't want her son to have any either, it seemed. The only friends she had were a few other spiteful women like herself, all of them also miserable old biddies who complained all the time.

Nobody would ever consider his mother a pretty woman and Virgil had always wondered why his father would have married her in the first place, but he supposed that was just one of the many things in life that he wouldn't ever know the answer to. Pa had never told Virgil why he picked her, but he seemed like he had liked her okay while he was alive... but his Pa had liked everybody. Virgil shrugged and got on with the job at hand.

Since his father's death, the Dare Lumber Company had allowed them to stay on in the house for no charge and given her a one-time death payment, which was almost gone now. Both of them picked up what work they could get, but things were tight and getting tighter all the time. She had developed a tendency to take all her spite out on him. *Just spreading her misery around*, he thought.

He vented his frustration on the woodpile. After filling the wood box and making a good-sized stack near the back door, Virgil quietly laid down the ax and took off running, ducking low so that she wouldn't see him out the window. He would deal with whatever she had to say to him later – right now he was going to get out of here and have a little fun!

When he reached the Mill Tail Creek landing for the shallow-draft boats, he saw his friends Sasha and Ryan standing together there, discussing something that seemed important; both their heads were bobbing and their arms were shooting out now and again in order to make a point. He walked up carefully, whistling a tune as he approached to give them a little warning.

Both of the young men turned when they heard him and immediately stopped talking. Their silence told Virgil that whatever it was they'd been talking about, it was evidently none of his business. He grinned at them and said, "Plannin' to get into some kinda trouble, fellas?"

They both glared at him. He stopped short, hands still in his pockets and stood there with a blank face. Finally, Sasha grinned back at him and said, "Da, skeenny boy, and do you think you might vant to get in on it with us?"

Virgil smiled but said nothing. Sasha was the son of some of the original Russian immigrants who had been brought in to construct Buffalo City in the beginning. The two of them had been friends since boyhood. Ryan was less friendly, but then he seemed to follow Sasha's lead as always and grinned at Virgil, too. Both of the boys were over eighteen and Virgil looked up to them, trying to tag along whenever possible.

"I'll go if you'll have me," Virgil said, laughing. "Just tell me how long I'll have to be in jail if it all falls apart, so I can git myself ready!"

Ryan gave him a dirty look but Sasha slapped him on the back. "You a funny boy, you know that, Vurgeel?" It seemed to Virgil that Sasha always put a bunch of extra 'e's in his name when he said it, but it was fine by him. Sasha tried hard to speak without a Russian accent, but correct sentence structure and the sounds of some particular English consonants were simply too difficult for him.

The girls all said that they thought Sash 'looked and sounded cute'. Ryan was nowhere near as good-looking as Sasha; his eyes were too close together and his chin was almost nonexistent. But hanging around with Sasha seemed to up his worth somewhat with the girls, so he almost never left the Russian's side because the girls were always following Sasha around.

Ryan spoke up. "We was just talkin' about going into business together, serious business. You want in?" He raised one eyebrow and stared Virgil down. Ryan was shorter than both Virgil and Sasha, but he was broad and strong, his thick, short neck connecting his somewhat small head to his massive shoulders. Ryan had the well-deserved reputation of being a mean fella that you didn't want to get on the wrong side of, so Virgil made an effort to keep their relations friendly.

Virgil cleared his throat, trying to think this through a little before he said anything one way or the other. "I can always use some extra money..." he said carefully. These boys were older and far more worldly-wise than he was, so he knew enough to be cautious when dealing with them.

Sasha threw his head back and laughed his big, loud laugh; then turning like a leaf in the wind, he got a serious look on his face. "You might not like vhat ve are talking about doing, Vurgeel," he said. "But there's no money to be made round here unless ve take us a chance of some kind. It's a small chance, but a big money that Ryan and me are discussing."

"If you ain't interested, you won't be tellin' nobody about it, right?" Ryan asked, scrunching his forehead, causing his eyebrows to move further away from his hairline, further enhancing his bad-boy look.

"Naturally! You know I can keep a secret as good as the next fella if not better!" Virgil said.

"Then come over here and seet down. Ve got us some serious talking to do," Sasha said, leading him to a bench nearby and taking a seat beside him. He looked over at Ryan and then at Virgil. "You know that lots of men here been making their money selling the liquor, don't you?"

"Sure," Virgil said, shrugging. "Everybody knows that. Ever since the logging 'round here has dried up, if it wasn't for moonshine, nobody'd have nuthin!"

Sasha nodded heartily. "Da! So Ryan and me has got us a good-sized boat. Ve plan on running some of the moonshine up to 'Lizabeth City and then filling boat back up with sugar for return trip. That way we make money coming and going!" He slapped his thigh and laughed at his own joke.

Ryan said in a neutral voice, "We could use another pair of arms for loadin' and unloadin' and makin' the trip, you see, and we thought of you. You want in on this or not?" Somehow Virgil heard a threat implied in those words.

Virgil swallowed hard. He was aware that a lot of men and women in and around Buffalo City were making their living on moonshine these days. But did he want to do that?

Since Prohibition, it had become increasingly difficult to keep all the liquor joints supplied with hard liquor, but the Buffalo City men had been increasing production and making their best efforts. They had come up with a quality product, labeling it 'East Lake Moonshine'. The folks in nearby East Lake seemed to take a certain pride in that.

In fact, 'East Lake Moonshine' was some of the best you could get and people now asked for it by name in speakeasies up and down the east coast; Virgil had heard that people in London, England, were even ordering it! Made with rye instead of corn, some men said that it was so smooth that drinking it was like drinking water – it had no bite at all, went down easy and was powerful stuff.

Because the taste was so mild, the 'Flappers' of the day called it *sugar rum* and mixed it liberally with anything they had; the men who provided them with it liked the results of that. As a result, it was in high demand and brought good money wherever you could sell it. But Virgil was keenly aware that The Law was always after the bootleggers and a not a few of them had been caught and taken away to prison.

"So you ain't talkin' bout makin' it, you just want to move some?" Virgil asked.

"Da!" Sasha replied, waving his hands. "We don't vant to spend all that time out in the voods with the snakes and the skeeters cookin' up the stuff, ve just vant to take it, unload it, and get paid on both ends! Sounds good, no?" Sasha's exuberant grin was infectious.

Virgil was growing more excited by the minute. Of course he needed money! He and his mother were barely scraping by on what he could pick up in odd jobs and she could bring in doing other people's wash. But if they got caught... well, it was a dangerous proposition.

But wait! Virgil realized suddenly. *They said they had a boat? How in the world did that happen? They were as poor as anybody!* "So what's this boat of yours like? Is it very big?" he asked cautiously.

Ryan nodded. "She'll hold enough for us to make every trip well worth our time. She's old, but she's steam-powered and can make some good speed. I figure that we can take at least a hundred gallons in one trip to Elizabeth City and a big load of sugar comin' back."

Virgil's eyes opened wide. A hundred gallons was a lot of moonshine! But it was also a lot of weight, and it would be hard to move at any speed carrying all that unless you had a big boat. But somehow it didn't seem wise to ask how his two poor friends had come up with a boat of any size, especially one capable of carrying that much. "Wouldn't it take us way too long to make the trip with a heavy load like that?" he asked. If he could only buy a little more time to think this over...

Sasha dismissed the objection by a simple shake of his head. "Nyet. Vell... maybe the first time or two. But then ve fly over the Sound, like the birds do!" Sasha moved his flat hand back and forth gracefully through the air to demonstrate his point. "Ve fly!" Sasha said, grinning from ear to ear.

Virgil liked that about his friend Sasha; he was often happy-go-lucky. If there was anything to laugh about, Sasha would find it. On the other hand, the big blonde Russian didn't always see things for what they really were, more for what he wanted them to be. And he could be downright scary sometimes, the way his mood would flip abruptly from good humor to anger when life didn't go his way.

"What you think, Virgil?" Ryan asked, crossing his arms, tilting his head and lowering his chin.

Virgil knew that the two of them could be trouble, but down deep he longed to be part of their group. "Well, I know that Ma ain't gonna like it, that's for sure," he said, shaking his head. "But then I might not have to tell her all the details if ya'll don't blab to nobody else 'bout what we're up to. Can you do that, you think?"

Sasha and Ryan shared a look that made the hair on Virgil's arm rise up. Then, changing quickly again, Sasha turned to Virgil and said, "Sure, skeenny boy, sure! Fewer people know, the better," grinning from ear to ear as he slapped Virgil on the back again. "Ve make the big money, no?"

Virgil inhaled and exhaled deeply. "Let me work out somethin' to tell my ma. In the meantime, I'd like to see this boat of yours."

"Da! Da! She a beauty, you gonna love her when you see her!" Sasha put his hands out and ran them over an invisible female body." You can put your hands on her and feel her all over if you vant!" he said, elbowing Virgil in the ribs and winking.

Virgil rolled his eyes and shook his head.

The three of them walked down the path beside Mill Tail Creek until they came to a sheltered spot near the shack

Sasha lived in with his parents and siblings. It was after dark by this time, but there was a full moon so Virgil could get a fairly good look at the boat, which was anchored there. It was an old, used-up-looking thing to Virgil, but seemed to be seaworthy. On the bow was written in block letters, 'Wilmington Woman.'

"This boat came from Wilmington?" Virgil asked casually.

"Don't matter where it come from, you idiot, it's ours now!" Ryan growled at him, causing Virgil to take a step back.

Sasha shrugged. "Anyway, ve be changing her name to 'City Queen,' you like that?"

Virgil snickered at the name and said, scratching his head, "Well, I do see that she looks sorta stable and all, but there ain't no way we could carry a hundred gallons on this old tub..." He'd been around boats a little more than the two older boys.

"Maybe we could get eighty?" Ryan asked.

"Da, eighty be easy," Sasha said, nodding.

The three of them stood there, arms crossed, studying the boat for a few minutes. Finally Virgil said, "Okay, I'm in. But we gotta do this careful-like. There's a few others doin' the transportin' and they ain't gonna like that they got more competition."

Ryan shook his head. "You worry too much, Virgil! There's more likker comin' out of these woods than they can ship. It backs up out at the storage areas where they hide it. I seen it myself! The men runnin' the stills need more shippers and not just anybody will take a chance on goin' to prison if they git caught haulin' the stuff, you know!"

"So, you come vith us?" Sasha asked him. "You skeenny, but we need another man so we can load and unload quickly. You the one ve vant. How about it?"

Virgil stretched his neck to the left and then to the right, and finally put his hand on the back of his head and rubbed hard. "Alright. I'll do it. Ya'll git the details lined up and let me know. I'll need to make up some story to tell Ma in the meantime."

Sasha grabbed him and lifted him in a big bear hug. "Vurgeel, you vill not be sorry! Ve all be big rich men soon! You'll see!"

Ryan stood with his arms crossed, glaring at the two of them.

"I just want to know one more thing..." Virgil said after Sasha put him down.

"Da, vhat's that?" Sasha said.

"How **did** ya'll git your hands on a boat like this?"

There was a long beat of silence during which Sasha and Ryan shared another look that made Virgil think twice about his decision. He knew that whatever their answer was, he wasn't going to like it.

"Don't you worry about how we got it, it's ours now!" Ryan said, adding, "Let's just say we won it in a card game. You are either in or out, which is it gonna be?" he demanded, leaning toward Virgil.

Virgil swallowed hard. "I...I... I guess I'm in, then," he sputtered.

Ryan nodded his head. "Okay. Then don't ask no more stupid questions that are none of yer business! This boat belongs to me and Sasha now and that's all you need to know!"

Chapter 7

Two weeks and a lot of hard work later, the boys were ready to make their first run. Virgil told his mother that he was going to do night watch work for a boat-builder who worked a few miles down the creek. She was not happy about it, but when he told her that it paid well, she grumbled and fussed but finally agreed. Nothing ever made the woman happy these days, so he settled for her reluctant permission.

The three of them met at the docks around dark. They walked to where the boat was tied up, got aboard and then started her up. The old girl's engine chugged and sputtered and sparked, but finally evened out. They headed down Mill Tail Creek toward the Alligator River.

"The *City Queen*, huh? I think that you over-named the old girl," Virgil said, hanging over the rail and keeping an eye on the propeller to make sure nothing got caught up in it. "She ain't much of a queen! We'll be lucky if she even makes it to 'Lizabeth City, much less back again!"

Sasha threw his head back and laughed out loud. He drove along for a few minutes, studying the shoreline in the dark. "The man that needs his likker moved has a place up here, but it is hard to find," Sasha said as they crawled along the curving creek slowly. After twenty minutes, they stopped at a particular place on the creek and Sasha did a birdcall. A few seconds later, his call was answered with one like it.

Tree branches were pushed aside and they moved the boat up a little tributary until they almost grounded. Three men had been watching for them, and a wagon loaded with five-gallon glass jugs filled with East Lake Moonshine stood waiting for pickup.

The oldest man approached them, holding a shotgun at a threatening angle. Speaking in a matter-of-fact tone, he said, "Now I know we agreed on all of this, Sasha, but I'm tellin' you right now that if you take this load and disappear, I will hunt you down and kill you like a mad dog." He spit tobacco juice onto the ground at the young man's feet. "You understand what I'm tellin' you, Boy?"

"Yes, sir," Sasha quickly responded. "Ve be back by dawn, vith your load of sugar and your cash. You can trust us!"

The bearded man in the ragged clothes put his hands on his hips. "You better hope so, Son!"

They nudged the boat in closer, threw down some planks to use as a gangway, loaded the jugs of whiskey by hand and got underway. The moon was just a sliver in the sky as they steamed down the creek and eventually toward Elizabeth City. "This is gonna be a long night," Virgil said, his heart racing.

"But ve make a lot of money!" Sasha said. "No more talking than ve have to now, the government agents hide out in these parts, so you two look and listen and I drive boat. Ve go fast and make no sound!"

Virgil smirked at that; this was a loud old tub and they could hardly sneak around in it, so they were counting on luck being on their side tonight.

A few miles more and Mill Tail Creek dumped into the Alligator River. The *City Queen* took off into the wider waters like she knew right where she was headed. With Sasha at the helm, the plan was to go straight there and straight back as quickly as possible.

The Alligator River dumped into the Albemarle Sound, a wide body of water protected on the east by the Outer Banks. They chugged along and made their way from there up the Pasquotank River.

They finally reached Elizabeth City, a good-sized port town up the Pasquotank River off the northern side of the Albemarle Sound. So far they'd had no problems; it was after one in the morning when they sighted a particular landmark. They cut the motor and drifted slowly up to the landing, a shabby looking dock in a rugged, hidden inlet of the sound. They listened for any sign of life at all, but could only hear the crickets and an occasional hoot owl.

Ryan was fidgeting. "Where they at, Sasha? They're supposed to meet us here, right?"

"They be here. You just vait," Sasha said in a reassuring manner.

After fifteen minutes or so, they heard a strange bird call.

"That's the signal!" Sasha said, and jumped out onto the rickety plank landing. He answered the bird call with one of his own.

Three men approached the riverbank slowly, shotguns raised in the air, one pointed at each of them.

"Who are you?" the largest man asked.

"Ve are your visitors from Mill Tail Creek," Sasha said.

"Okay," the man responded, having received the signal he was looking for. "We'll bring the wagon down close to the dock. This old dock'll never hold up for us to drive the horses and wagon up on it. First we got to unload your likker onto the ground, then we unload our sugar onto the boat and then ya'll help us git the likker up on the wagon. Ya'll git started with that and we'll bring the wagon up as far as we can."

All six of them formed a chain, passing the heavy, five-gallon glass jugs marked "East Lake Rye Whiskey" at a good pace. They worked silently and soon the moonshine was unloaded and the sugar was loaded in its place. They turned to loading the heavy jugs onto the waiting wagon. Before long, the job was done.

Sasha looked at the big man and said, "The sugar is only part payment for the 'shine. Where's the rest of our money?"

Sizing up the three of them, the man said, "Look here, boys," then spit on the ground. "If you can deliver us this much or more on a regular basis, then we got us a business arrangement. But that there bucket of yours don't look like it's gonna hold together even to get you back to where you come from. What you plan to do about *that*?"

Sasha stood up to his full height of six foot three inches. "Ve are putting the profits from the first few trips back into the boat. Ve vill make bigger, stronger engine and fix up the rest of it." He gave the man a determined look and held out his hand for the cash.

The man shook his hand instead. "Name's Edgar. You can call me Mr. Ed, everybody else does."

Sasha shook his hand and then stuck out his hand palm up once again.

Edgar laughed. "All business, you Russians," he said, shaking his head. "But that's fine by me 'cause this is business we're doin'. Here's your cash." He handed a wad of bills to Sasha, who counted them.

"Mr. Ed, you a good man to do business vith," Sasha said, grinning. "Vhen you want to get your next load? Ve can deliver at least a hundred gallons each trip, maybe more."

Edgar nodded. "That's good then, it'll all work out fine. We'll make it Wednesday night next week, and then Tuesday night the following week and Thursday the one after that. Then we'll go back to Wednesday and keep up that same schedule. You got that?"

"Sure," Ryan spoke up. "Wednesday, Tuesday, Thursday, Wednesday, Tuesday, Thursday. No problem. You can get us the sugar we need?" Ryan asked.

Mr. Ed nodded and grinned. "All you want and then some!"

"See you next Vednesday, this same time, then. Good to do business vith you!" Sasha stuffed the cash into his pants pocket, turned and headed back toward the boat, Virgil and Ryan following close behind. The men boarded the boat, started the engine and headed south down the river toward the Albemarle Sound. Once they were well underway, Sasha turned to the others, grinning widely.

"See? I told you! Big money, no problems!" he said, patting the bulge in his pocket.

Virgil exhaled loudly and felt a little of the tension leave his body.

Ryan asked, "So how much of that cash is ours?"

"Vell, ve got to pay the man who makes the likker with the sugar and part of the money, of course, and then ve take a fourth of what is left for the boat, and a fourth for each of us. But, like I told Mr. Ed, the first profits go back into making our boat run good. Then ve get rich!" he said, slapping Ryan on the back.

Virgil scratched his head and frowned. "You didn't say nothing to me 'bout puttin' our profits back into the boat! How long we got to do that?"

"Just till she is running smooth — maybe two, three trips. Vithout boat, ve got no business," Sasha said. "Ve baby her along so she make us the first trips and then ve fix her up real good!"

Ryan, who evidently was aware that there was no money to be made at first, nodded. "It's just good business, Virgil. We got to have us a reliable boat to make money. Me and Sasha, well we're the ones who got the boat in the first place, so you have to go along with it!"

Feeling that things were moving along without him somehow, Virgil turned on the two of them. "And just where did you git this boat from, anyhow? Ya'll didn't have the money to buy a boat! It wasn't no card game, was it? You never did tell me the story," he asked, hands on hips.

Sasha and Ryan looked at each other. Ryan looked away, leaving the explaining to the big guy.

"Ve didn't exactly buy the boat, ve just... ve found it!" Sasha said, steering the boat along into the darkness and not looking Virgil in the eye.

Virgil took a moment to absorb that. "What?! *Found it*?" He looked confused for a moment until a realization hit him. "You mean *you stole* it, didn't you?" he sputtered.

"No! We... found it, it was abandoned..." Sasha said.

Virgil wasn't having it. "Nobody abandons a boat that runs and ain't full of holes!" he said, waving his arms. "Where in the world did you git it?"

Ryan stepped over and put his hand on Virgil's shoulder, clamping down tight. "Don't worry, Virg, ain't nobody gonna come lookin' for it, you can be sure of that."

Virgil's eyes got as big as possible; he backed away from Ryan. "You didn't kill somebody and steal their boat, did you? I ain't gittin' involved in no murder and boat-stealin', you hear me?"

Sasha gave him a serious look. "Like Ryan said, do not vorry about it. Ve made a deal with a man who... vas in trouble. Ve got him out of trouble and he gave us the boat in payment. That is all. The boat belongs to us now. But if you vant out, you don't have to go again; Ryan and me can do this."

Virgil walked over to the port side of the boat and leaned on the rail. Steam was coming out of the engine, which was hitting and missing and chugging and sputtering, but still seemed to be making fair time. Their story made no sense at all, but the thought of that big wad of money was more than he could resist. He took a deep breath, shook his head and turned back to the other two men.

"Okay. I'll keep working with you, but if I git wind of anybody 'round here bein' killed or havin' their boat stole, I am gonna git as far away from you two as I can!"

Sasha smiled. "Nobody gonna report stolen boat or dead body, I promise you that." He looked over at Ryan, who nodded and then smiled slyly.

Virgil made the rest of the trip in silence. The other two whispered between themselves a little. By the time they made land at the small dock where the moonshiner unloaded his sugar and took his share of the cash, everyone was laughing and slapping each other on the back, so Virgil began to relax a little.

Maybe this would be a good arrangement, after all... and perhaps Sasha and Ryan really *had* come by the boat without having to steal it...

Chapter 8

Two months later, the young men had managed to put enough cash back into their business to get the boat running smoothly. They'd made eight successful trips and were now in business for a profit. Fortunately they had encountered no government agents, called locally 'Revenooers', or run into trouble of any kind; in fact, they were starting to get a little cocky, Virgil feared.

"Seems like a good night for makin' the trip," Ryan said, looking out over the Sound. The stars twinkled brightly overhead in a clear sky.

"Da. Not much moon. Good thing," Sasha agreed, nodding his head.

Virgil peered cautiously out over the dark water. He was still quite anxious each and every trip, but the other two had begun to relax and even have a little fun on the way home. It seemed to Virgil that they weren't taking it seriously enough, but then he was new at this kind of thing and younger, so he couldn't be sure and didn't feel right calling them out on their behavior. He heaved a sigh.

As they approached Elizabeth City, they slowed to a crawl along the shore, getting their bearings on their location and then heading toward their prearranged meeting site. Suddenly, they heard a man's voice call out to them from the trees along the shoreline.

"What ya'll doin' out there so late at night?" the deep voice hollered.

Sasha looked at the others and took charge.

"Ve only fishing!" he yelled back.

"In the middle of the night, are you crazy or sumthin?"

"Just now coming in!" Sasha called out. "Vat you doing out here yourself?"

The voice went silent for a long moment. "None of yer business, that's what!"

"Den ve go about our way, and you go about yours," Sasha yelled, pushing the boat a little faster to get past the nosey man. That was the last they heard from him, but it woke up both Sasha and Ryan to the possibilities.

"You think he'll tell anybody 'bout us?" Virgil asked Sasha.

"Nyet. He is probably up to no-good himself and just vanted to make sure ve was not the Law or anything…" Sasha said, shrugging his shoulders.

Virgil was suddenly wary. This was the first time they had made contact with anyone who wasn't directly involved with their business. The brief encounter now made him realize just how vulnerable they were, what easy prey they would be for either the revenue men or perhaps others who might want something they had and feel like taking it.

"How we gonna protect ourselves if we meet up with trouble, Sasha?" he asked.

Sasha looked straight ahead. "Ve got a gun."

Virgil's eyes widened. *A gun! Where'd they get a gun?* The bad feelings were starting to mount up for him, like a load that was getting too heavy to carry. There were so many unknowns; and he was not the kind of man to take easily to this illegal way of life. He considered asking where the gun had come from, but decided instead to let it drop. There was a lot going on here, and some of it he simply didn't want to know about because knowledge brought with it responsibility.

The rest of that trip proceeded without incident, as did the next few.

One night as they steamed down the Alligator River from Mill Tail Creek, they heard a boat gaining on them and saw lights flashing over the water in the distance. They knew they were being pursued by the law, and the patrol boat was coming up fast. "Now we go to emergency plan!" Sasha called out and stopped the boat.

The plan was simple: The twenty five-gallon jugs that they were carrying had been tied together by the handles, one every six or seven feet hung along four lengths of rope, which they called a trot line. Every long rope pulled five jugs and had a small float attached to the end. They picked up the first jug on each of the bundles and lowered them carefully one at a time over the four corners of the boat. Then they circled back around to end up between the oncoming patrol boat and where they'd just been. They cut the engine and waited.

The larger boat belonging to the Coast Guard shined several lamps on them. "Stand down to be boarded!" was shouted over a megaphone.

When the agents got on board, all they saw was three young men, one in the wheelhouse and two more innocently fishing off the side of the boat. Ryan, who had pretended to fishing, looked up and asked in a confused voice, "What's goin' on?"

Sasha laid down his pole and walked up to the officer. "Vhat can we do for you, sir?" he asked politely.

"We're searchin' this boat for illegal liquor, that's what's going on!" he said, turning to Ryan, who was now getting up. "And you three had better stay put right where you are and make no funny moves, you understand?"

"Sure, officer," Virgil said, raising his hands and looking frightened without having to pretend. "But we ain't got nuthin' like that on our boat!" He glanced around slowly, making sure there was no sign of anything having to do with the liquor trade.

After a thorough search, the officer confronted Sasha. "We heard there was a new boat makin' runs between Buffalo City and Elizabeth City, and we figured that you were it. What are you boys doin' out here in the middle of the night?"

"Ve are fishing, sir," Sasha said innocently. "Yes, ve are from Buffalo City. Ve are trying to help our families get by because the logging in Buffalo City town is not so good anymore. So ve try to make a little money by taking out my uncle's boat, catching fish to sell, helping to feed our big families."

Looking around the officer said, "Uh-huh. You're a far piece out from home to be *fishing*. How's it going, you catching anything?"

Sasha shook his head. "Not yet. Ve are just getting started tonight, had to work all day and then sleep just a little before ve come out. Vhat kind of fish you think is running good right now?" he asked, tilting his head. "You got any suggestions for us? Ve are new at this and not very good fishermen!" He shrugged and gave the man a self-deprecating look.

The man studied the three of them and seemed to relax a little. "Well, drum is running and I hear they're catching some amberjack out in the ocean, but let me see what you're using for bait and maybe I can offer a tip or two..."

Sasha spent the next fifteen minutes seeking the expert opinion of the Coast Guard officer and thanking him for his help. Then the men re-boarded their vessel and got back underway, waving to the boys as they left.

When the boat was out of sight and could no longer be heard, all three of them let out deep breaths.

"Well, that vasn't so bad," Sasha said with a big grin.

"Good thing you made that fishing plan ahead of time, Sasha, huh?" Ryan asked, rubbing his chest nervously.

Sasha grinned. "It vork like a charm, no? Ve are just three boys out fishing for our families!" He snickered. "You okay Vurgeel?"

White as a ghost, Virgil whispered, "I thought I was gonna pass out from fear! I think I even peed my pants a little!"

Sasha slapped him on the back and doubled over laughing; Ryan was laughing so hard that he had to grab the rail to keep from falling over. Virgil was embarrassed but then he, too, began to laugh. The raucous laughter seemed to ease a bit of their tension.

Sasha pulled himself together and wiped his eyes with the back of his hand. "So ve go find our 'catch' and get back on course, then?" he asked.

They all agreed, started the boat and slowly headed north again. It took a while to spot the floats in the dark, but when they found the first one, the other three were close by. Using a long pole with a grappling hook on the end, they snagged the rope and then carefully hauled in the jugs tied to their lines.

"Whew! That was a lot of work!" Virgil said, collapsing on the deck when they finally got it all back on board. "Did we lose any?"

Ryan shook his head. "Nope. Looks like one of the jugs got a lil' crack in it up by the neck, but it didn't leak. We was real lucky!"

When they floated up to the dock the next morning and explained why they were so late getting back with the cash, the moonshiners got a big kick out of their story. The boys got a little extra cash that night for their inventiveness. The story of the jugs on the trot line made its way around and soon all the bootleggers were tying their haul up like that, ready to throw it overboard at a moment's notice, cut it loose if necessary and then come back and get it later when it was safe.

The boys were now officially bootleggers, professional liquor haulers, or rum-runners as they preferred to call themselves.

Chapter 9

The three young men began to bring in some real money as the months went by, and were now making up to three runs a week. One night after they'd offloaded the moonshine and then loaded up the sugar, Sasha headed the *City Queen* toward town and then pulled up to a dock in Elizabeth City. He told Virgil to stay with the boat while he and Ryan went out exploring.

"What do you mean – exploring?" Virgil demanded. "We got to get back with this sugar! What if somebody sees us?"

Sasha patted him on the shoulder. "Hauling sugar is not illegal, Vurgeel," he said, patiently. "Ve can go back in daylight with this load and nobody can do nothing. Ve just vant to look around a little and spend some of our money," he added, grinning. "You stay here and vatch the boat." He turned to Ryan, signaled and they headed toward the dock.

"But what'll I do if somebody comes?" Virgil asked, looking all around him. "It'll be daylight in a few hours!"

"No problems, just act like you belong here," Ryan said, waving back over his shoulder. "We'll be back soon, just want to look around and see the town a little, that's all."

Virgil stood helplessly and watched them walk off; they headed toward the few lights still burning in Elizabeth City. He had a bad feeling about this; especially since the two of them seemed to have had it planned and didn't let him in on it until the last minute. But there was very little that he could do about it, so he decided to keep watch and wait.

A couple of hours later, the two returned arm-in-arm, laughing and singing. They had obviously been drinking, and now Virgil was really worried. They had to get back home and he wasn't even sure if these two would be able to get themselves onto the boat, much less drive it. They stumbled back onboard, laughing and falling over the edge.

"Well, did you *explore*?" was all Virgil could think of to ask.

They looked at one another and burst out laughing. "Da!" Sasha finally answered. "Ve saw some new places we never seen before!"

The two of them laughed so hard that they fell down on the deck.

"Ya'll are disgustin!" Virgil said. "You better be able to help me get this boatload of sugar back home and off the boat, or I'll pitch the two of you overboard when we get to the Sound!" he added, loosening the moorings and making ready to get underway.

That seemed to sober them up a little. They stumbled around the deck and set about getting ready to depart. They offered no argument when Virgil informed them that he would be driving the boat. About halfway home, Ryan threw up over the side and then fell asleep on deck. Sasha was able to hold it together, and by the time they reached Mill Tail Creek he was sobering up somewhat.

Virgil was over the worst part of being mad by then. He looked at Sasha and asked, "So, did ya'll just go drinkin'? That was your idea of 'looking around' the place, 'exploring'?" he asked with a sneer.

"Da," Sasha said, rubbing his face. "Da. Ve just go drinking a little, that's all you need to know about." The look he gave Virgil silenced the other questions that he'd been intending to ask.

"Well, don't you leave me like that again!" Virgil said. "I was scared and didn't know what had happened to you."

Sasha gave him a look of pity, as one might give a frightened small child. Then his face changed suddenly to fierce anger. "You vill not be telling me vhat I do and do not," he growled, turning away.

Virgil had seen his friend behave this way many times in the years he'd known him. Sasha in a good mood was usually the one who was the good-natured leader, the power behind their new business. This, however, was disturbing and a little bit unnerving because 'angry Sasha' was totally unpredictable; if he fell apart, there would be no business.

"Well, please take it more seriously, Sasha! We got a lot of time and money tied up in what we're doing here and it's dangerous business!" He pleaded with his eyes.

A bit of the old Sasha resurfaced. "Da, skeenny boy, not to vorry. Ve do okay and not get in trouble." He turned away and walked to the far end of the boat, staring out into the water.

After that run, Virgil thought seriously about quitting. The money was good, but he didn't really want this kind of life. One day he told his mother that he was considering giving up the night watchman job.

She stood working at the sink, dishrag in hand and said, "You're what?"

"I'm thinkin' 'bout giving up the job, that's all," he answered, relieved to be talking to her back.

She threw her rag in the sink, turned back around and put her hands on her hips. "You realize that I ain't gittin' any younger, don't you?" she demanded. "The money you been bringin' in has made it so that I don't have to work so hard as I used to, and I don't want to go back to scrubbin' other folks' dirty old clothes all day. My hands were so sore I could hardly bend em!" she said, flexing her fingers for him to see. "Just now I am able to move them without pain – you got any idea what's that like, Boy?" She gave him a look that removed any doubt from his mind. She was not going to let him quit.

He stared at her, feeling cornered. "I didn't know..."

She sat down across from him and laid her hands out on the table, palms down. "You cain't quit, Virgil! This is the first decent work you ever had. Your pa's gone and it's just you and me now. I'm gittin' old and you're my only survivin' child – it's your job to take care of me in my old age – you know that, don't ya?" She glared at him.

Virgil swallowed hard. If he quit, she'd never give him any peace. But if he told her what he was really doing, she'd thrash him alive. "I can git another job, Ma," he said hopefully.

"You ain't never had no decent job before and there ain't no more to be had 'round here – you know that! The best timber round here's all been felled and the company's about to go under! Whoever this boat-builder is that you're workin' for has got you workin' some crazy hours, but at least we got some money now! Who is this man, anyhow, you never told me his name? I know most everybody 'round here. What's his name?" she demanded.

"You know all the white folks, Ma, but you don't know all the Russians. He's Russian, and he keeps to himself. He builds small boats that he sells to local folks and he needs me to keep an eye on things at night so nobody makes off with his tools and stuff. You don't know him!" The lie rolled off his tongue but stuck in his craw.

She eyed him suspiciously. "Is he connected with the likker trade?" she demanded. "I don't want you havin' nuthin' to do with that stuff! They'll haul you off to prison and there won't be nobody left to take care of me!"

Trapped. He would have to continue working for Sasha and could see no way out of it. He lowered his voice. "I...I don't know who he sells his boats to, Ma, and I don't care. It's none of my business. I see a few people comin' and going' from time to time but it's understood that I don't ask questions, and you can't ask any either!"

She raised one eyebrow and glared at him. That was about as close to back-talk as he'd ever given her since he was little. "What you hidin' from me, Virgil?" she asked quietly.

His face reddened; he'd never been a good liar. He stood up, slapping the table as he rose. "Nothing, Ma, nothing! Just git off my back! I'll keep the job and take care of you til you die, don't you worry 'bout it!" He turned and walked out, having gotten the last word with this woman for the first time in his life.

Virgil stuffed his hands in his pants pockets and made his way through town to try to walk off some of the frustration his mother caused him. He studied the place as he went; *Buffalo City... some city*, he thought. A railroad was used to move the heavy loads of logs around and also in from the woods; the tracks ran smack through the middle of the main road all the way to the lumber mill. The roads themselves had been laid with reject lumber, poles and sawdust – so, depending on how much rain they'd had recently, you could be walking on warped wood or bogged down in a soggy mess.

At one time, it had been the largest settlement in Dare County, but since the lumbering work had fallen off, more people were moving out than in. It was rumored that there were still Indians out on the outer islands, and piracy hadn't died with Blackbeard back in the 1700's. This was rough, wild, marshy country, with the surrounding woods full of bears, big gators, and flies that seemed big enough to carry off a small child. It was a lot like the Wild West towns he'd seen pictures of; but it was all he'd ever known.

Once you got past the few businesses, on one side of the tracks were the red houses, where the white people lived and on the other side were the white houses, where the colored folks and Russians lived. *Kinda funny, when you think about it; black people in white houses and white people in red houses,* Virgil thought. *Oh well, there's no trouble as long as everybody minds their own business.*

The place had been founded in the 1870's not long after the Civil War, by the East Carolina Lumber and Timber Company of Buffalo, New York. The mill and houses were constructed mostly by Russian immigrants and African-American laborers brought in to do the work. Later it was purchased by the Dare Lumber Company, who put in a pulp mill.

Over a hundred miles of railroad track had been laid through the woods to bring in the cut trees. They'd hack all the best trees down and then move on, laying small-gauge track spurs anywhere they needed them to get to the cut-down trees that couldn't be skidded down to the water and floated in.

Since then the population had peaked at around 3,000 in the early part of the twentieth century. They had a post office, a general store, hotel and all the signs of a thriving community for many years. But the timber industry was not doing as well these days, as the best of the cypress timber had been felled and taken to market, so the population of Buffalo City was also dwindling.

Now the loggers and skidders, the same men and mules that had cut and dragged the timber out of the woods, were making the moonshine and hauling it to the boats standing ready to take it to market. Prohibition had created a big demand in illegal whiskey, and East Lake Moonshine was a hot commodity.

The high quality of the product produced was such that all the best speakeasies on the east coast were now placing orders asking for it by name; they couldn't make it fast enough. So logs and lumber had been replaced as the primary income-driver for the town, now famous for its smooth rye whisky.

Most of the residents there didn't ask and wouldn't tell if the subject came up; they were either making, selling or distributing it themselves or had some family involved. People did what they had to do to survive. They worked hard and felt that they earned every penny they made. The fact that it was illegal was neither here nor there. Even the local preachers turned a blind eye, leaving the future prospects of those involved totally in God's hands.

Just about everyone was in on the system; there were lines strung across the creek with children watching them to give warning of any unexpected boats. The system of runners and signals they had devised was ingenious and the revenuers never made it far up Mill Tail Creek without somebody knowing that they were on their way.

Virgil strolled past the Dareforest general store, where they sold anything and everything you would need out here in the backwoods of the low country. Most men were paid in "pluck", or tokens from the lumber company; those tokens could only be spent at the company's general store or traded to others who would spend them there.

The hotel, the other small businesses, together with the town hall, school and post office, made up the rest of the downtown area. Streets ran parallel to the main road behind the businesses on both sides of the road; most of the residents lived there in town or close by. Children attended the two-room schoolhouse until they had to be put to work. Virgil was able to go through the sixth grade before his mother took him out, so he could read and write fairly well, and was good with numbers.

Heavy snows came every winter; sometimes it would be hip-deep. The large pot-bellied stove in the center of the company store served the dual function of heating the place and providing a convenient gathering and gossip center for the men of the town as they huddled together for warmth. In warmer weather, that same bunch moved out to the store's porch or under a big shade tree nearby. They dragged their overturned buckets, small barrels and creaky straight chairs inside or out, depending on the weather. A weathered wooden rocker, arms split down the middle but smooth from wear, was reserved for the oldest man among them, who spent his time telling tales and doling out hard-earned wisdom.

Virgil never thought much about leaving; he'd been born here. But the way things were going, he knew that sooner or later the town would go so far down that there would be no future here. It was already nearly impossible to raise a family here – at least legally. And, too, his mother couldn't do other people's laundry when she got old; he had to admit that she was right about that.

At some point the responsibility for providing for the family had shifted to Virgil's shoulders, and his days as a boy were now over. He was eighteen years old and already deeply involved in the illegal liquor trade. He shook his head, wondering how such drastic changes had come about so quickly in his life and without his even seeing them coming! He didn't think much about getting married, but if he ever wanted to do that, this pitiful town was no place to bring a wife!

What was he going to do? What kind of future could he look forward to? He stopped and looked in the window as he passed the hotel. A few people were in the café there eating and talking. Looking at his own reflection in the glass, he saw the strained expression there. This 'becoming a man' was not an easy job, and he'd rather just go back to the carefree days of his boyhood.

But as a man he also understood that time was a lot like Mill Tail Creek itself; it only runs in one direction.

Chapter 10

"Ma, the man I work for wants me to move down there and stay in the little shack he built. It'll save me the long walk back and forth every night, so I'm gonna do it." Virgil looked up from the stew he was eating to gauge her reaction.

Her head snapped up. "You cain't do that, Virgil – I need you here! Who's gonna haul my water and chop my wood if you leave? And what about money? You know I cain't git by without what you bring in!" She cast a challenging glare his way.

He exhaled loudly. If only once his mother would say that she loved him, or would miss him if he left, that would be all it would take. But no, his Ma only cared about what Virgil could do for her. It seemed that after Pa was killed in that mill accident, something inside her had died along with him and was never coming back.

"I'll still come into town a day or two a week and do the chores you need doin', Ma," he said. "And," he added, before she could get the next words out of her mouth, "I'll still bring you money."

"How much?" she asked, squinting her eyes.

"Well, enough to keep you goin'," he said. "I won't let you do without, don't worry."

She looked off into the distance. "It won't be the same around here without you, Virgil..."

He tilted his head and smiled hopefully at her. "I'll miss you, too, Ma, but like you said, I got to keep this job 'cause I won't find another one round here nearly this good."

She stared at him and got a hard look on her face. "I didn't say I'd *miss* you boy, I just said things would be different without you," she said in a hateful tone of voice. "There'll be a lot less work cleanin' up with you gone, less cookin' and everything. I might even be able to get a little rest some days..." She turned her face away. "I've worked hard all my life and it's high time I was able to take things a little easier..."

Tears came into his eyes, but he shut them tight and willed the tears away. "Yeah, Ma, you do that," he said, getting up from the table. "You do that!"

"Where you goin'?" she asked sharply.

He glared at her. "Does it really matter, as long as I don't come back and bother you?"

She lifted her chin. "Don't go gittin' all mad about it, I was just saying that..."

"I know what you were saying, Ma! I'll git your work done and bring you money, don't you worry! And you won't be doin' no cookin' nor wash for me, neither! I'll be the perfect son, one that's never here!" He smacked his dish down on the wood planks by the sink and walked out, slamming the door behind him.

His mother looked after him for a few long minutes and then lifted the tail of her apron to wipe her eyes. "Men…" she said softly. "They're all alike! Sooner or later they'll leave you high and dry!"

Virgil had already discussed with Sasha the possibility of living on the boat. The idea sounded good to the Russian and also to Ryan. They both lived with their big families and were content there, but it would be a definite plus to have someone living onboard and protecting their investment.

So he moved the few possessions he could call his own onto the boat. Sasha had named her the *"City Queen,"* though they'd laughed about it to begin with because she wasn't very regal. In fact, even with the improvements they'd made, the *Queen* looked far more like a hungry peasant. Over the next few days, Virgil built himself a makeshift bed in the small cabin and got hold of a kerosene burner to do what little cooking he did. For the most part, he ate fish, hard-tack and panbread, together with the occasional rabbit or squirrel he managed to catch or trade for.

On the one hand, Virgil's life was definitely more peaceful. His mother seemed almost glad to see him whenever he came into town bringing money, and usually made him a hot meal. They were getting along much better now that they weren't living under the same roof. He was making more and more money, but didn't really have much to spend it on, so he'd begun to put it away in a little box kept hidden under his bed on the boat. After the first year, he had accumulated quite a tidy sum.

Now it was the summer of 1932, he had turned nineteen and his mind was drifting toward his future and a certain girl he'd met. If he could only save enough, he could move his mother and himself to someplace like Elizabeth City, where he could then get legal work and set them all up. But it would mean living in the same house with her again, so he wasn't in any hurry to make that happen.

Sasha and Ryan had finally decided to let Virgil have his turn at 'exploring' when they docked at Elizabeth City. He'd discovered the world of grown men, including bars and women, but he wasn't that fond of liquor and the women he'd met scared him a little. After you got to know them, you realized that all they were really interested in was your money and would do whatever they had to in order to get hold of it.

They had scheduled runs to Elizabeth City twice a week and were now making a once weekly trip to Manteo, as well as an occasional trip further down south to Ocracoke Island. Ocracoke had become Virgil's favorite place; the quaint little fishing village with its history of piracy was a different kind of place. It seemed to him that when he was there his pressures were fewer, time seemed to slow down and everything looked a little brighter, more peaceful somehow.

He'd met a girl there named Lillian back in the spring. Of course, she didn't know exactly what it was that Virgil was delivering when his boat docked, but then Lillian was smart enough not to ask too many questions. The folks who lived on Ocracoke Island were definitely of the live-and-let-live variety. It was a place as primitive as Buffalo City in many ways, but the community seemed more like a big family to Virgil than a bunch of strangers thrown together.

Virgil had noticed that the village appeared to be divided into two sections; people there called themselves either 'Creekers' or 'Pointers.' He discovered that everyone to the north of the creek that cut deeply into the little island was a Creeker, and everyone south of there out toward the point was called Pointers. As small as the island was, the two groups didn't seem to mix any more than they had to.

That was almost laughable to Virgil, who'd grown up in a town made up of whites, colored folks and Russians, who managed to all get along fairly well together. These Ocracoke people all looked and talked just the same but still managed to divide themselves off into 'us' and 'them.' He pointed that out to Lillian, who was a Pointer, but she didn't seem to understand that Creekers and Pointers were all just alike to anybody from outside the island.

Lillian's father, a friendly fisherman named George Dows, had been kind to the boys and had invited them to their home a few times. Her mother was welcoming and had been happy to feed the three hungry men. Lillian was the oldest of seven children, so a few more around the table didn't seem to make much difference to her mother. Mrs. Dows seemed to Virgil to be the kind of mother he'd always wanted; she usually gave him a hug and smiled a lot at the three of them, especially him. Sometimes they'd stay the night and sleep on the boat, so he'd get to see more of Lillian.

Virgil liked to think about Lillian; in fact, he thought about her often these days. She was so sweet, and her long blonde hair hung in ringlets, even though she tied it back with a ribbon most of the time. She wasn't what Ryan or Sasha would call beautiful, but to Virgil, she was more appealing every time he laid eyes on her. She was smart and not too sassy – just enough to keep him on his toes.

He'd asked Sasha if they could increase their Ocracoke runs to twice a month, and Sasha explored the possibilities on their next trip down there. It turned out that the folks there would indeed be interested in having twice as much Buffalo City Moonshine delivered, and they made a deal.

Virgil and Lillian felt an immediate attraction and soon developed a friendly relationship. They became relaxed in each other's company and quickly fell in love. However, her father had by this time discovered exactly what it was that the boys were delivering and took Virgil aside to have a little talk with him. They sat by the docks on overturned buckets, looking out into the small bay that was called Silver Lake.

"Virgil, it's plain to see that you're interested in our little Lillian," the older man said.

"Yessir, Mr. Dows, you could say that," he answered, swallowing hard. "In fact, I was planning to talk to you about that before too much longer..."

George lifted a finger. "Before you say anything else, let me talk plainly to *you*, Son," he began. "I know what you and the other two are haulin' on that old bucket you call a boat." He held up his rough, calloused hand to stop Virgil from saying anything. "Now, I didn't say I disapprove, 'cause I believe that every man does what he has to do to get by in this world, but *you* doin' that and you draggin' my little girl into it with you is two different things, don't you think?"

Virgil hung his head. "Yessir, and to tell you the truth, I been thinkin' about gittin' out of it for a long time now." He looked up to see her father nodding his head in approval. "And I got me some money put away so's I can git us a real good start somewhere else. I know a lot of men in Elizabeth City now and I could git me a good job there, I'm sure. I really don't like this kind of work..."

Mr. Dows looked at him for a long time. "Virgil, I don't believe that you could lie to me if you wanted to – you got the kind of face that won't let you git away with it." He laughed.

Virgil reddened, thinking of all the lies he'd told his mother. Well, he *was* working for a Russian man... and he *was* living in a shack (on a boat). But lying to his Ma had been one of those 'must-lie' situations – there simply hadn't been a way around it!

Mr. Dows went on. "And besides that, I pride myself on knowing men, and there's a lot of good in you, Son. That's why I been willing to let Lillian go 'round with you all this time and have not put a stop to it. You're respectful, you treat women good – like a man ought to treat 'em – and you got a good head on your shoulders," he said putting his hand on Virgil's arm. "But I'd hate to see my little girl married to some man who was off in prison and not able to take care of her and her children. That just wouldn't do at all!"

Virgil hung his head and nodded.

George wrapped his arm around the younger man's shoulders and gave him a brief squeeze. "You git yourself out of the likker business, Virgil, and we'll talk more about you and Lillian. I could probably make a fisherman out of you and find you some work on a boat 'round here, cause you're good with boats and fishin' here is serious business." He got a sad look on his face. "But if you got to take my little Lillian off, then Elizabeth City ain't that far away, I reckon..."

Virgil smiled broadly. "No, sir, not by boat, it ain't!"

Mr. Dows lifted one side of his mouth in a wry smile. "Son, this here is an island. Only way to git anywhere from here is on some kinda boat!"

Chapter 11

Two days later

The big Russian waved his arms around. "Nyet! You cannot leave us, Vurgeel! It is too much vork for me and Ryan, and ve need you to live on the boat to protect it!" Sasha was clearly upset; everything had been going so well for them, and they were beginning to make what he called 'the big money.'

"Now settle down, Sasha, I ain't talkin' bout leaving today! Maybe another six months or so, anyway. By then you can git somebody else lined up to make the runs with you. Lots of fellers need money these days."

"But no feller like you..." Sasha got a sad, hurt look on his face that made the big lug look like a little boy who had lost a puppy.

"You don't understand, Sasha! I love Lillian and want to marry her and have a home and young'uns and all! Her father won't let me even *ask* her, as long as I'm in the likker business! And besides that, I don't want to be worryin' all the time about bein' caught and took off to prison for a year and a day like all them other fellas that got caught!"

"Ve not get caught, skeenny boy, ve are too good at vhat ve do!" Sasha said, ruffling Virgil's hair.

Sasha hadn't called him a skinny boy in over a year now, so Virgil had to grin. Nowadays he was nearly as tall as the big Russian and had filled out to be quite bulky. Hauling moonshine not only paid well, but the work was hard and required lots of heavy lifting. Virgil had become a man in every way.

Virgil shook his head slowly. "Six months, Sasha. That's all I got in me for this work. I ain't suited to breakin' the law like you and Ryan are! I got me a sweet little gal who I hope will marry me, and I plan on doin' just that." He crossed his arms and stared at his friend.

"Me and Ryan can get you a girl anytime you vant one, you don't have to get married!" Sasha made a face and lifted his hands palms up, as if this were no problem at all.

Virgil lifted one eyebrow. "Uh-huh, I've seen the kind of girls ya'll bring out onto the boat, and I don't need none of that! I got me a good girl, and I don't want the trashy ones ya'll hang around with!"

Sasha looked mildly offended to begin with, but then shrugged and grinned. "That is the kind I vant right now," he said. "Maybe someday I find me a good girl, too, but now I vant to have fun with all kinds of girls!" He elbowed Virgil in the side. "And that is just vhat I am doing!"

Virgil shook his head. "I reckon that would be your decision to make, Sasha. All I ask is that you let me make my own."

Sasha stuck out his massive hand and they shook. "Okay, skeenny boy, ve give you six months and then ve look for replacement for you. And *then* ve go to your wedding!" He slapped him on the back.

Chapter 12

Two weeks later

Late one night after unloading the whiskey and loading the sugar, the three young men docked the *City Queen* at a slip at the main port in Elizabeth City; Sasha and Ryan left to go do what Sasha called 'splorin' and Virgil waited onboard, thoroughly disgusted with their behavior. The two of them had already been drinking and were well on their way to being useless.

Virgil shook his head and busied himself with the boat. Before long they returned and brought two girls back with them; it had become a routine for them. But Virgil noticed that these girls looked awfully young, and they were doing more than a little laughing. Evidently the boys had been feeding them the sugar rum.

All four of them were downright pickled, that was easy for Virgil to see. *I'll be out of this soon*, he thought. *Til then I'll just have to put up with it...* But after closer inspection, he saw that these two didn't look like the usual hussies that they brought on board for fun, but more like girls that came from good homes. That worried Virgil, so he took Sasha aside.

"Sasha, them gals ain't your usual barflies and tramps," he said pointing toward the two giggling girls now talking to

Ryan, "that kind got daddies who would hunt you down and kill you! Git those girls off this boat, we don't need that kind of a problem! We got to go on back! Please, Sasha..." he pleaded.

"Nyet! They told us if ve take them out on the water that they vill have a little fun vith us!" he said, raising one eyebrow. "You vant us to have fun, don't you?" he asked, swaying from side to side. Sasha's eyes looked glazed over, so standing up straight and speaking simultaneously seemed more than he could accomplish.

Virgil grabbed hold of the big guy to steady him. "I just want to get back home and get this trip over with! And those two girls don't look like the trashy kind you usually bring back," Virgil said, challenging the older boy. He pointed toward the two young girls. "They're too young, can't you see that? Girls like them can get you into real trouble, and I don't want no trouble!"

Sasha's face turned grim. "Look, this is *my* boat and **I say ve are taking the girls out for a ride**. Girls are girls, and all of them out at this time of night vant the same thing! You just drive the boat out a'ways, drop anchor and mind your own business! Ve vill bring them back after a little vhile and then ve go home!" He gave Virgil a little shove back, stared him down, then turned and walked away unsteadily.

Ryan introduced the two of them as Rose and Linda. Virgil mumbled something and got busy with the boat, reluctantly agreed and then raised anchor, heading away from shore. Not too far down the river Ryan signaled to him;

he stopped the boat and dropped anchor. It was a pleasant night, so Virgil went back into the wheelhouse and closed the door, leaving the four of them outside on the deck. He lay down on his little bunk and tried to take a nap, ignoring the noises from outside. This had become a pattern with the two of them, and he didn't like it one bit! Soon, he told himself, he'd be done with all this business!

Just as he relaxed enough to doze off lightly, Virgil was awakened by the sound of hysterical screaming. He jumped up, opened the door and things started happening fast: he saw Ryan slapping one of the girls, Rose, and cursing at her. The other girl, Linda, coming to her friend's rescue, jumped onto Ryan's back and began to try to choke him; both of the girls were screaming their heads off. Sasha staggered over and tried to stop the melee, but then it turned into a full-blown fight, with Ryan trying to get one girl off his back while the other pounded him on the chest and about the head with her fists. Sasha was grabbing and stumbling, trying to get his balance and get ahold of the girl on Ryan's back at the same time.

As all this was taking place a large swell passed under the boat, causing Sasha to lose his balance. The four of them went down in a pile, the big Russian on top, with the screaming and cursing continuing. They rolled around a bit, scuffling, grunting and grabbing, and then one of the girls screamed extra-loud.

"She'd dead! Rose hit her head and she's dead!"

The free-for-all came to a sudden halt. Sasha lifted the screaming girl off Ryan's back; the one under him had stopped moving. There was blood flowing freely from a deep gash in her head. She had obviously come down head-first onto an iron cleat on the deck as they had fallen, and the weight of the other three had caused the force of the fall to drive the point of the cleat right into her skull.

"*My sister – you killed my sister! Rose, Rose, are you still alive?*" the first girl cried, pushing both the boys away and lifting her sister's head gently into her lap, crying and moaning and carrying on. She looked up at them. "You killed my sister! Rose! Rose!" She continued to moan and wail and carry on loudly.

"It was an accident!" Ryan said, waving his arms about. "She hit her head when we all fell and it was *an accident!*"

Linda turned to Ryan, a look of hatred flashing in her eyes. "You was slappin' her 'round – I saw you – that's why I jumped on you! You were gonna beat her to death, I could see that!" the hysterical girl shouted. "You murdered her! You murdered my sister!" She lowered her head to her sister's and cried loudly. "*Rose! No, no, Rose, don't die!*"

Virgil pulled himself out of his stupefaction and stepped out of the wheelhouse. "Let me look at her, maybe she's just knocked out," he said gently, lifting the sister's hand from Rose's head. The blood had been pouring out and Linda's skirt was soaked with it. But the flow had slowed to just a trickle now. He grabbed a rag and held it against the wound. With his other hand, he felt her chest to see if her heart was still beating.

"Don't you touch her! You dirty stinkin' man, all you want from us is to touch us! Git your hands off my sister!" There was a crazed look in Linda's eyes as she reached out and violently flung Virgil's hand off her sister's chest. He backed off and stood up, looking at Sasha and shaking his head slowly. There was nothing to be done – the girl was definitely dead.

The three boys stared at one another, horrified. Suddenly Linda looked up at them and said through her tears, "You will all three pay for this!" She gently laid her sister's head on the deck in the pool of blood. Rose's blue eyes had rolled back in her head, so Linda carefully closed the lids. She stood up and put her hands on her hips. "You take us home right now! You're gonna pay for what you did to my sister!" she screamed at them.

"I didn't do nothing!" Virgil said. He pointed toward the wheelhouse. "I was laying in there asleep! I ain't goin' to jail for something I didn't do!! Please – I didn't do nuthin'!"

Ryan stepped forward and growled, "Ain't nobody going to jail – it was an accident! You don't go to jail for no accident!"

Linda looked at him and stuck her finger in his face. "You slappin' her around wasn't no accident! If you hadn't been beatin' her, this would never have happened. It's all your fault!" Her sobbing had turned now to a fierce anger. "I hate you! You'll pay!" She glared at each of them in turn. "You'll all pay!" My daddy will see to that! You killed my sister Rose and all three of you will pay!"

Ryan fumed and his face turned red. "Ya'll promised to have some fun with us, and when I tried to lay your sister down, she got all hysterical and started screaming. I was just trying to slap some sense into her, to get her to shut up, that's all! Then you jumped on my back and I lost my balance and fell on top of her! I didn't beat her head against the deck or nuthin! I didn't kill her!"

Linda raised herself up on her toes, reached back and slapped him hard. "Our daddy runs the Mercantile in town! We're good girls – we didn't come out here for that, we just wanted to go out on your boat and have a little excitement; we snuck off and didn't tell nobody we were goin' out, but when my folks find out what you've done, you'll pay! You murderer! You killed my sister!" She began to pound on Ryan's chest, screaming bloody murder the whole while.

"Shut her up, Ryan!" Sasha said. "Ve are not that far from shore, somebody's gonna hear her screaming! Shut her up!"

Ryan grabbed both of Linda's wrists, holding them in one of his large hands. He tried to calm her down, but she only screamed louder; he covered her mouth with his hand and she bit his finger. So he hauled off and punched Linda in the face; her eyes rolled back; she melted against him, unconscious.

"Oh my god, Ryan, what have you done?" Virgil cried, reaching out to help him lay Linda down beside her sister. He looked up at the other two and grabbed his head. "What are we gonna do now? We'll go to prison for sure! I told you not to bring them girls onboard! Oh, God, what's gonna happen to us?"

Both Ryan and Sasha were cold sober by now. They looked from one to the other, shaking their heads. Sasha was the first to speak. "Ve'll all hang for this! Ve got to get rid of these girls... drop 'em off somewhere..."

Ryan shook his head. "I'm skeered to death of hangin! Their Pa is *somebody* here, we cain't let that other one talk... She said they snuck out and nobody knew it. Nobody saw us with 'em, we were careful about that. We cain't let *that one* tell *nobody*..." He glanced at Linda and gave Sasha a knowing look.

It took Virgil a long moment to process what the other two had just said. "What are you talkin' 'bout?" he demanded. His mind was racing but he couldn't make any sense of what was going on through the confusion of his naked panic.

Sasha shrugged and nodded. "Ve got to get rid of the bodies. Nobody saw them get on our boat, so nobody can connect us to them..."

Virgil exploded, pushing Sasha back and flailing his arms about. "What do you mean, *bodies*? Only one of 'em is dead, the other's just knocked out cold!" He pointed to the two limp forms sprawled on the deck.

Ryan and Sasha exchanged a look. Ignoring Virgil's outburst, Ryan said to Sasha, "We can tie 'em up with rope and tie that rope to the anchor. That should sink the bodies to the bottom and nobody will ever find 'em! Their folks'll just think that they run off or somethin'! We'll stay away from town for a few weeks and nobody'll ever know we had nothin' to do with it!"

Virgil turned and grabbed Ryan by the shirt. "But she's not dead!" he shouted frantically, pointing to Linda. "That would drown her – we can't do that! Are you crazy?!"

Sasha came up from behind him and jerked Virgil back so hard that he fell over the girls and lay sprawled on the deck beside them. Sasha leaned over him and said, "Linda is the only one who can tie us to Rose's death – ve have to get rid of her! Ve got no choice! Right, Ryan?" He turned to Ryan, who looked ready to come back at Virgil and tear him apart.

Ryan stared at them, the look on his face as cold as ice. He took a deep breath and, wiping his palms against one another, finally said, "He's right, Virgil, we got to get rid of 'em or they'll hang us all. If we take 'em back to 'Lizabeth City, Linda will tell who did it and we will *all* go down for it!"

"But I didn't do nothin'!" Virgil cried out again. "I'm innocent, I *didn't do nothing*!" He stood up, holding out his hands pleading with them. Tears began to pour from his eyes.

Ryan exploded on him, waving his arms. "Do you think that'll make a hill-of-beans wortha difference with a jury of twelve men who see a dead girl and her poor hysterical sister? Use your head, man! If these girls live, we all die, so we got to decide right now which it's gonna be! Sasha's right – we got no choice! It's us or them! What's it gonna be?" He moved threateningly toward Virgil. "I ain't gonna let 'em hang me – no way!"

Virgil's heart was pounding in his chest and he felt as if he couldn't take a deep breath. He rubbed his hand over his face and then over his whole head, moaning and shaking his head. "I cain't kill nobody, 'specially a girl! I ain't never killed nobody, and I ain't about to start now! I ain't no **murderer**!"

Ryan turned to Sasha, nodded toward Virgil and raised an eyebrow; Sasha appeared to be considering things. Virgil caught the exchange and swallowed hard. Understanding that his own life was now in jeopardy, he looked to his friend Sasha to save him.

Sasha walked over and put his hand on Virgil's arm. "You don't have to do nothing, Vurgeel. Ryan and me vill take care of it. You just go back in the cabin and ve tell you after it is done. Go, now!" The look he gave Virgil caused him to tremble with fear.

Virgil meekly complied and went in and shut the sliding door. He faced the bow of the boat and didn't turn around.

All the while his head was pounding and he could feel his heart beating in his chest. *This wasn't right!* But if he tried to stop them, they'd just kill him and dump his body, too, and he knew that for a fact!

Out on the deck, Ryan put his hands on his hips and looked down at the girls. "How we gonna do this exactly, Sasha?"

Sasha picked up a piece of rope and bent over. "I think ve should tie the two of them together, and then tie the other end of that rope to the anchor and toss them over. That should do it, don't you think?"

Ryan scratched his head. "Both of them together, like in a bundle?"

Sasha nodded. "I think so. Neither one comes lose and floats off like that..."

"Okay, then. Let's, uh – stack 'em up, like, so we can run the rope under 'em." Ryan bent down and picked up the hands of the unconscious girl. "You grab her feet."

"Turn her over so they are face-to-face, Ryan. Good. Now run the rope under to me." He took the rope as Ryan slid it under the bodies and brought it up and around, handing it back to the other man. They did this several times until they felt the two were tied securely, arms pinned to their sides and legs bound together. They heard a low moan and Sasha said, "Quick, Ryan, she's coming to, ve got to work fast now! Pick them up!"

They lifted the heavy bundle and stood the girls upright, dragging them over to the side of the boat where the anchor was kept. The boat had never had a real metal anchor; what they had been using was basically just a large, heavy rock tied up and attached to a long rope. It usually took two of them to lift the rock, but so far it had held the boat securely in place in wherever they'd stopped.

Linda was coming around and began to moan more loudly and wiggle a bit. She was growing louder by the second; the boys tried to work fast.

Ryan said, "Hurry, Sasha – we got to git this done!"

They quickly tied the rope securing the bodies to the end of the rope attached to the anchor. Sasha and Ryan lifted the heavy rock and heaved it into the river, then turned and picked up the girls as the coils of rope unfurled from the deck. Just as they lifted the bodies over the rail to toss them overboard, Linda opened her eyes wide and looked straight into the bloody face of her dead sister. She turned her head and stared up at both of them. She screamed one last time as the men threw them into the water.

Virgil heard the scream and turned just in time to see the girls go over. He would never forget the sound of the splash their bodies made when they hit the water.

They went in feet-first and as the rope tightened they began to sink. Sasha and Ryan watched them begin to go under, ever so slowly, their long hair fanning out on top of the water. Linda was screaming and gurgling until she was totally under, and then only bubbles came up. Eventually those stopped as well.

After a few minutes Sasha yelled at Virgil that he could come out. The boat drifted a little; the three men watched the water for a long time, not looking at one another. Then Virgil rushed over to the other side of the boat and threw up, retched and threw up again. He dropped to his knees, still holding onto the rail. He began to cry, silently at first and then out loud.

Sasha let him cry until he was done and then said, "Let's go." He told Ryan to start the engine and they headed south into the silent darkness.

Ryan steered the boat toward home, his reflexes on automatic, their many trips over these waters helping him to sense where all the obstacles might be and make the best time possible. Not a word was exchanged between the three of them during the entire trip home. As they pulled up to the inlet to deliver the sugar, Sasha said, "Now ve got to get our story straight. Ve didn't see nobody or talk to nobody tonight. Ve just delivered our load and then came home. Everybody got that straight?"

Ryan nodded and said, "Nothing unusual happened, right Virgil?" and looked over into Virgil's white face, glaring at him.

Virgil swallowed. "I don't know, fellas... them girls are dead..." He couldn't look either of the other two in the face.

"Don't we need to tell somebody or do something?" He was trembling from fear for both the dead girls and himself.

Sasha took two long strides over to Virgil and shoved him roughly back against the wheelhouse. "Nyet! Ve tell nobody nothing! If ve get involved in any way they vill know it vas us and ve will hang! *Can you not see that it is us or them?* And *they* are already dead, ve are still alive!" He slapped his own chest to illustrate the point.

The thought of the two girls' bodies floating near the bottom of the Sound, their faces looking at one another in death, brought a sick feeling to Virgil again. He ran over to the edge of the boat, but this time nothing would come up, only the scratchy sounds of retching.

Sasha waited until Virgil turned around and said to Ryan, "Get ready to dock, then tie us up to a tree onshore. Ve vill unload this sugar, make the payment and go home. Let Virgil stay in the cabin; if anyone asks, ve vill say he is sick."

Ryan nodded and got to work. Virgil slowly made his way over to the wheelhouse, collapsing onto his small bed. He turned toward the wall, buried his face in the dirty pillow and began to cry as quietly as he could. He heard the sound of the boat docking, the sugar being unloaded and the muted conversation between the men, as if it were all going on in a dream. Finally Sasha started up the engine and the boat began to back out of the small creek into the open water of Mill Tail Creek.

As they steamed toward home a cold, dreadful feeling washed over Virgil. He was afraid that he would now be living an awful nightmare, one that would never end and from which he'd never awaken.

Chapter 13

The cold, dark water was perfectly still until the bubbles starting coming up; one or two at first and then dozens of them were surfacing. Two bodies, tied together, suddenly bobbed to the surface and began floating around, both of the girls with their faces turned to the side, cheek to cheek, looking straight at him with pure hatred in their eyes as they opened their mouths to scream, "You killed us, you killed us, you murderer!"

Virgil awoke from the dream, trembling. He sat up in bed quickly, throwing off the blanket, and then looked around. It was still dark but just before dawn; the sound of crickets was all he could hear. Getting his bearings, he realized that he was aboard the *Queen*, sleeping on his narrow bunk in the wheelhouse as usual. He rubbed his hand over his face and then through his hair. Sweat was dripping down his neck despite the chill in the air.

Virgil got out of bed and went to the back of the boat. He reached way down and splashed his face and neck with the water from Mill Tail Creek. Looking up, all he could make out was the fading sliver of a new moon. His body ached and his stomach was sore from all the vomiting he'd done.

Standing there, he recalled every little detail of what had happened the night before. He shook his head as if to dismiss the reality of it; but he couldn't get the sound of Linda's screams and gurgles out of his mind. Tears ran down his face and he collapsed onto his knees, sobbing silently. Sasha and Ryan had gone home as if it were any other night; cold-blooded murder had been committed on innocent young girls and they hadn't seem to let it bother them...

Virgil sat on the deck of the *City Queen* with his head in his hands, feeling alone, empty and scared. He was not a religious person normally; all the hypocrisy he'd seen made him believe that if there was a god, he wasn't to be found in the small church in Buffalo City. But at this particular moment, he needed to pray to somebody or something...

"Dear God, whoever you are, I am so heart-sorry for what we done last night!" he said aloud, closing his eyes. "Even though I didn't do nothing myself, I didn't stop it from bein' done, so I reckon I'm about as guilty as the others. I might could've saved one of those girls, anyway... they'd a'prob'ly killed me too then, but at least I would've died with a clean conscience."

He lifted his head, swiped his wet cheeks with his shirttail, and looked up. "But God, I promise you right here, right now that I'll never intentionally hurt another human being as long as I live! And I sure won't murder nobody, you can count on that!" He glanced upward to see if there was any sign he'd been heard. Only the sounds of the river and the woods could be heard, but he took that as a good thing in itself. Life would go on. The creeping dawn seemed to offer him the promise of a future that might be a little brighter...

No more tears would come for Virgil. He washed his face, dressed and went to find Sasha. He met him on the trail as morning was breaking full over the treetops.

"Good morning, Vurgeel," Sasha said pleasantly. "Be a nice day, no?"

Virgil stopped, put his hands on his hips and glared at the big Russian. "Nice day? Is that all you can say after what happened last night?!"

Sasha shrugged. "Vhat else? It vas a terrible accident, but as they say, 'accidents happen,' my friend. No one vill ever know that ve vere involved. The, uh, bodies will never be found."

Virgil waved his hands around. "You can't be sure of that! It was all done in a hurry and helter-skelter-like and who knows what might happen down there at the bottom of the Sound! They could float up anytime!"

Sasha approached him cautiously, laying a big hand on his shoulder. "You didn't do nothing, Vurgeel, it was not your fault. What happened is on me and Ryan. You just forget about it." He squeezed Virgil's shoulder extra-hard before letting go and lowered his voice, looking him in the eye. *"You vill forget about it, da?"*

Virgil swallowed hard. Who knew what the big guy might do to him if he felt threatened? He realized that he might easily 'disappear' if he tried to cause any trouble for these two! He took a step back. "Well," he began, "I cain't live with it, and I don't want to work with ya'll no more! I'll keep my mouth shut, but I want out of this deal we got – and I want out now!"

Sasha sized him up before speaking. "Tell you vhat, Vurgeel. You give us two more veeks and then you can go. Ve need to find somebody to take your place, and it needs to be the right person. This is a three-man job."

Virgil looked away. That seemed like a reasonable request, and if he wanted to stay on Sasha's good side – which he did – he could do that much. They would need a couple of weeks of watching him closely to make sure that he was going to keep quiet. "Okay, two weeks and then I'm gone."

"And you vill never talk about what happened? You vill be hung just like us if you do, you know... Vhat's done is done and telling people von't change it!" Sasha squinted at him.

"I promise. I will take the secret to my grave!" Virgil said.

Sasha laughed. "Hopefully you vill be a smart man and live for long time yet, no?" He gave Virgil a look that the younger man didn't quite know how to interpret.

Virgil simply nodded.

"Okay, then, let's get to vork on the *Queen*! She needs some extra attention after vhat ve put her through with that run last night!" Sasha said, turning Virgil around and heading him back the way he'd come.

The two of them walked together with no further conversation and got to work on the boat. Cleaning up the bloodstain took a long time, but finally they scrubbed most of it up and Sasha declared that the rest would look like fish blood. After an hour or so, Ryan turned up, walking toward the boat.

Sasha jumped onshore, met Ryan on the creek bank and walked, putting his arm around Ryan's shoulders and steering him away from the boat. They talked in hushed voices; at first Ryan looked upset, but after enough talking, Sasha got him quieted down and even had him laughing before he was done. The two of them climbed aboard and got to work.

"Mornin' Virgil," Ryan said casually.

"Mornin' Ryan," Virgil spat.

The next two weeks would not be easy.

Chapter 14

One week later

Immediately after they unloaded in Ocracoke, Virgil went to find Lillian's father. After shaking the older man's hand and greeting him, he said, "Mr. Dows, is that offer to teach me to be a fisherman still good?"

George Dows tilted his head, thought for a long moment and then said, "You gittin outta that business you're in, Virgil? And I mean, *all out*?"

"Yessir. All out. Forever."

Dows nodded. "And what about Lillian, son?"

Virgil swallowed hard and worked up his courage. "I'd like to have your permission to marry Lillian if she'll have me, Sir." He lifted his chin.

George laughed. "Oh, she'll have you; I'm sure 'bout that part at least! You're all she talks about anymore! The sooner we git the two of you hitched, the sooner she'll stop her blabberin' 'bout you!"

Virgil grinned. "I hope not, Mr. Dows; I hope she blabbers on about me for forty or fifty more years!"

He smiled and slapped Virgil on the back. "You're alright, Son, you're alright! If you'll do for my Lillian, then I reckon you'll do for me and her ma! So when can you start working with us?"

"I got another week to work out on my notice with the Russian. Then I'm free. But I need to find a place for me and my Ma to live here on Ocracoke Island. We have to git out of Buffalo Springs if I'm going to be working with you. And I promised my Ma that I'd take care of her til she died, so I gotta get her over here with me."

George nodded. "You're a good boy, Virgil. I'm sure we can find something, or throw something together, for ya'll to live in. In the meantime, you and your mamma can stay with us."

Virgil grinned. "Mr. Dow, I appreciate that offer, but it's like this: my Ma is a real hard woman to be around, and I'm purty sure that you don't want her in your house with your family. I need to git me and Ma set up somewhere and then we'll talk about me and Lillian gittin married. I got me some money saved up and can afford to build us a little place somewhere if I can find a patch of land."

"We got land, Son, and Lillian's mamma will be happy to have ya'll nearby since you're takin' her away from us," he said, smiling. "We'll work something out. But there's one more thing you gotta do first, Son," he said, shaking his finger in Virgil's face in a serious manner.

"Yes, sir, what's that?" Virgil asked nervously.

"You gotta ask the girl!" Dow said, slapping him on the back again and heading him away from the docks and toward his own house, laughing loudly.

When they walked up in the yard, Lillian was outside hanging wash on the line. She spotted Virgil and ran to meet him, stopping just short of throwing her arms around him. He smiled, took her by the hand and said, "You and me need to take a little walk, Lillian, if it's alright with your pa..." They glanced at her father.

George nodded and shooed them away with his hand. "Git it over with, the sooner the better," he said, shaking his head and laughing. "I'm goin to talk to her ma." He headed toward the back door of the house.

Squeezing her hand, Virgil led a confused Lillian toward the shade under a big live oak tree, its lower branches bent nearly sideways by the constant wind. He put his hands around her waist and sat her up on one of the low branches, moving in close.

"Virgil! What you doin?" she said, nervously glancing back toward the house and pushing him back gently.

"Well, it's like this, Lillian..." he said, looking serious and rubbing his chin. "I got me a big problem and there's only one way out of it that I can see..."

She reached out to him. "Virgil, what's wrong? What's happened? Are you alright?" she said, scrunching up her face.

Virgil gave her a pitiful look. "Well, right now I'm pretty bad off, but I will be just fine and dandy if you'll say that you'll be my wife…" He grinned at her.

Her facial expression slowly transformed from concern to confusion and then to joy. She jumped down off the branch and threw her arms around him. "Oh, yes, Virgil, yes, yes!" she said, and then kissed him right on the lips out there in front of her parents and God and everybody.

Virgil held Lillian tight and released the deep breath he wasn't aware he'd been holding. He was going to start a new life. Everything was going to be alright.

Chapter 15

Buffalo City
One week later

"You quit your good job? To be a fisherman? Are you crazy, boy?"

"Ma, I'm getting married and you're not talking me out of it!" Virgil put his hands on his hips and looked down into his mother's eyes. "You can holler at me from now til doomsday, and I ain't changin' my mind! The only question now is: are you comin' to Ocracoke to live with us, or are you gonna stay here in Buffalo City?"

His mother's face was beet red and she began to flail her arms again, yelling "I ain't goin' nowhere! I'm stayin' right here at home and you're stayin' with me! You can bring that gal here and she can live with us! I been here most of my life and I ain't about to leave now!" She pointed her finger at him. "And you cain't make me move to that god-forsaken little island that gits hit by every hurricane that comes through!" She crossed her arms and sat down, turning her face away from him.

Virgil shook his head and rubbed his chin; he had known that this wouldn't be easy. "Alright then, Ma, if that's the way you want it, then you can stay here. But I'm moving to Ocracoke!"

She snapped her head around. "You cain't leave me here all by myself – how'll I git by? You ain't gonna support me here from over on that little bit of an island, are you?" She shook her head. "No! I'm stayin and you're staying with me!"

"Stay if you want, but it'll be mighty hard on you here... Me and Lillian will take care of you if you live with us on Ocracoke, but I ain't obliged to support you unless you'll live with me." He picked up his cap and set it on his head. "It's your decision. I'm goin' over there today to start buildin' us a house, and if you decide to come, send me a message by one of the boats. Goodbye, Ma." Virgil walked quickly toward the door, opened it and left.

As he was trotting down the steps he heard his mother say, "You can go to blazes, boy!" He didn't slow down or turn around, but just kept walking.

A week later Virgil's four-room house was starting to take shape. Mr. Dows and many of the other men on the island had been volunteering their free time to help him build on a pretty spot not too far from the Dows' house, across the marsh from the lighthouse.

The Dows had been feeding Virgil, who'd been sleeping on a friend's boat. In just another week or so he'd have the place all dried in and could sleep there himself. It would be a few more weeks before it would be fit to live in, but when it was he and Lillian would be getting married.

Virgil stopped to drink some water from a bucket, looking back at his very own home. Four large rooms were a beginning. And like every other house on this island, they'd add on as the need came. He would build a little shack for his mother across the yard and get her out of Lillian's way, hopefully. His life had taken a turn for the better and he was beginning to come out from under the depressing feelings that he'd had as a result of his moonshine work. *Never again*, he promised himself. *From now on, I'm never doing nothing illegal!*

Within a month of starting construction, Virgil moved his meager possessions into his new home. The folks on Ocracoke had taken him into their hearts and been generous with the few things that they had; he now owned a bed, an old cookstove, a rickety table and two chairs, and a chest for clothes. He knew that he could put together whatever else they would need in the evenings after working on the fishing boat with Mr. Dows.

He and Lillian set the date for their wedding one week later. Mr. & Mrs. Dows were wholeheartedly in support of that, because the two young people couldn't stay away from one another and they knew that getting them married would be the only remedy for that. Virgil sent his mother a letter, inviting her to the wedding, but didn't hear anything back.

The day of the wedding came and Lillian walked down the aisle of the little island church looking a vision of happiness; her cream-colored muslin dress was decorated with beautiful embroidery and a touch of lace here and there. She wore a wreath of flowers in her hair and joy radiated from her lovely young face.

Virgil considered himself a truly blessed man; his life had turned around. As he watched her walk toward him, he almost broke down in tears, but made himself man-up and stand straight, shoulders back. However, his ear-to-ear grin couldn't be repressed.

The joy of their wedding supper was shared by all the friends and family on the small island, and they told Virgil that now he was officially an "O'coker."

He laughed and leaned over to Lillian to ask what an O'coker' was.

"Why silly boy, it means you're one of us – an Ocracoker, or O'coker for short!

He grinned and nodded. That's what he wanted to be – an O'*coker* and a fisherman and a husband. He was a very happy man.

After a long weekend together, Virgil had to leave his Lillian to go to work on the boat, which would be his new life. He found it to be a lot like running moonshine, but much harder work. Being out in the hot sun fishing was not quite the same as flying across the water at night, then turning and making the trip back loaded with sugar. But he enjoyed his life and his marriage to Lillian was the greatest source of his joy.

Virgil's mother had not been seen nor heard of, and though Virgil worried about her, he knew that she would only come if and when she was good and ready. Until then, he and Lillian would settle in and then deal with that problem when it walked through the door.

Chapter 16

Elizabeth City, North Carolina
November, 1932

"Did you hear 'bout Charlie Strout's two girls gone missin' for so long now?" one pock-marked ne'er-do-well asked another as they sat on a gray, weathered bench out by the docks.

"Yep."

Not getting the enthusiasm for gossip that he'd hoped for, the first man continued, "Well, I just heard that his wife is 'bout to go crazy for worryin' for them lil' gals. They was both as purty as you'd ever like to see in these parts, too!" He turned his head to see if that statement would elicit a more enthusiastic response.

The other man made a rumbling noise deep in his throat and then spat his tobacco for at least eight feet – an impressive feat in itself – but said nothing in reply.

The first fellow wasn't giving up. "Ain't you curious 'bout what happened to 'em? I heard they run off with some men myself; but then I also heard that they caught a ride on a boat and went on up to Norfolk..." He titled his head, thinking that maybe his companion was either deaf or not right in the head.

After nearly a minute's silence, the second man slowly turned his head toward the first and said, "The way I see it is this: it ain't none of my business, and probably none of your'n, neither." He stood up and ambled off toward the bar.

Shaking his head, the man on the bench muttered to himself, "Some people jes ain't got no imagination nor curiosity neither..."

The entire town of Elizabeth City had not only heard the tale of the two missing sisters, but had also formulated any number of possible scenarios about what might have happened to them. A massive search had turned up nothing. Since they had been known as good girls who were silly but never got into any serious trouble, the theories ranged from running off to stay with their grandmother in Norfolk without telling their parents, to the less believable one of running off with two boys. But as of yet there was no sign of them.

No one had seen them leave the house the evening of their disappearance. As far as their parents and siblings knew, they were safely tucked into bed for the night. Unbeknownst to their parents, their little adventures of climbing out the bedroom window and sneaking off to do whatever looked like fun had begun just a week earlier, but the two girls had been a little braver and bolder each time they sneaked out.

The night that they met the handsome Russian and his friend was the first time they had ever been alone with boys; it was also the first time that a drop of liquor had ever passed their lips; so needless to say, the effects of the boys' smooth Buffalo City moonshine hit them hard and fast. They had first become giddy, then pliable, and finally reckless, which had started the unlikely chain of events that had ultimately led to their deaths. So no one in town had any clue about what had really happened to them; they had seemingly disappeared without a trace.

"Amos, if you don't find my girls, I'm gonna have to git somebody in here who knows what they're doin!" the angry man hollered as he slammed his fist down on the old wooden desk, causing a few loose papers to fly around.

The sheriff leaned back in his creaky chair and stared up at the red-faced man. "Now, Charlie, I understand that you're worried 'bout them girls, but you got to leave this to me, you hear? I been askin' questions from Norfolk to Ocracoke and ain't nobody knows nuthin', so that in itself tells me two things."

Charlie Strout planted his fists on his hips and leveled a stare at the sheriff. "Like what?"

"Well, it tells me that they probably don't want to be found, for one thing. Most of the time runaways are trying to scare their folks, so they make a big deal of telling all their friends what they're doin' so that somebody will come find 'em. Then their mamma and daddy go lookin' for 'em, find 'em and then when they git home they either git what they wanted or they git their tails beat."

Charlie glared and shook his head. "Everybody knows that my girls wouldn't run away, Amos! They just disappeared from their beds one night and you and me both done talked to everybody who knows 'em. And don't nobody know nuthin'!"

"Right. So that tells me the *other* thing, and that is that they prob'ly run off with some fellers and so they'll be gittin' word to you real soon that they're married and livin' somewhere else. They figured that they couldn't git your permission, so they just eloped. It happens, Charlie." He shrugged.

The big man shook his head. "Nope. They wouldn't do that. They were good girls, and you know it! They wasn't seeing no boys or men, all their friends will tell you that!"

It was the sheriff's turn to shake his head. "Even good girls fall head over heels in love and run off now and then, it happens!" He laughed harshly.

"To the both of them at the same time?" Charlie demanded, growing redder in the face. "No, they had better sense than that! And there wasn't no boys involved, I'm tellin' you! Besides, all the boys around here are accounted for!"

"Well, their bedroom window was up and there wasn't any sign of a break-in, so they must have left of their own accord. You and Nelda need to just settle down and wait, they'll turn up. More'n likely, they'll come back soon bringing you some grandbabies..."

Charlie Strout leaned forward, putting both his palms flat on the desk and breathing heavily. "I outta flatten you for saying that, Amos Graham! You don't deserve to wear that star! You just sit here on your butt and pretend to solve a few minor crimes once in a while, but you are no kind of lawman!" he spat.

The Sheriff stood up, pointed at the door and yelled at him, "You git outta here right now, Charlie Strout! Them girls will turn up, you just wait and see! In the meantime, you stay outta here 'cause I don't want to see your ugly face again!"

"Since it's clear that you ain't gonna do nuthin', then I *will* have to git somebody else!" Charlie shot back.

"Like who?" the sheriff scoffed.

"Just you wait and see, Amos, just you wait and see!" He turned on his heels and walked out in three long strides.

"Huh!" Amos said to himself, "everybody thinks they know my business!"

Chapter 17

Norfolk, Virginia
Three days later

Lucky O'Rourke sat in front of the window in his sparsely furnished office, straining to read the scribbling on a letter that he'd just received. Whoever had written it had been either in a big hurry or highly agitated – that much was clear. He squinted and read on.

Finally he was able to make out that it was a plea for help from the father of those two girls who'd disappeared recently down in Elizabeth City. The news of the missing girls had gotten around so that everyone within a hundred miles had heard of it. He'd seen a photo of them in the newspaper; their innocent faces were stuck in his mind.

The father was understandably distraught. Evidently he'd decided that the local sheriff was inept because he'd been unable to find them or any clues about what might have happened to them. And Lucky knew that with every passing day the likelihood of finding those girls dwindled...

Letting the letter fall to the floor, Lucky rubbed his big hands over his face; he was hoping to get away from this kind of business. Ten years of working for the Pinkerton Detective Agency had given him more than enough time solving *that* kind of case; kids ran away all the time and most were never seen again because they didn't want to be found. *But normally they weren't girls from good homes, especially sisters, and these two were awfully young, just sixteen and fifteen*, he told himself reluctantly.

He'd read all the newspaper articles about the case: Their father, a man of fine reputation, owned a large mercantile store in the port town of Elizabeth City and had offered a hefty reward for their recovery. *These girls were probably spoiled and looking for attention... but then, they should have turned up by now if that were the case...*he thought, struggling with the idea.

Bending over to pick up the letter, he read through it one more time, feeling the weight of both the message and the heavy paper between his fingers. "No sir, I'm not doing any more cases like this..." he said aloud to himself. "Nope, no more cheating husbands or runaways!"

He shook his head for emphasis, but couldn't get the picture of those young girls' faces out of his head.

Two days later Lucky found himself driving into Elizabeth City in his old, beat-up 1921 Model-T Ford. It's true, business had been very slow and he'd found that trying to set yourself up as a private investigator wasn't as easy as he'd supposed it would be. But still, it had its advantages.

Nowadays nobody told him which cases he had to take and which ones he couldn't... but people were still leery to hire a man from 'somewhere else', despite the fact that he had been both a Baltimore policeman and a Pinkerton Detective for all those years.

He hung his long arm out the window and signaled a left turn. Spotting the mercantile, he chugged to a stop out front. He grabbed his hat and straightened his coat and tie; then he got out of the car and walked up to the store.

The bell on the door tinkled as he opened it. Inside he found himself surrounded by an amazing array of items for sale. Any kind of household implement you'd ever need was either on display on a shelf, stacked up somewhere or hanging from the ceiling. Lucky smiled; the place reminded him of the store near where he'd grown up just outside Baltimore.

Charlie Strout looked up from the counter where he'd been counting spools of thread and saw the man enter the store and look around. *Probably another city-slicker down to go fishing for the day*, he told himself. Taking a deep breath, he looked the man over. Charlie noticed the scar on the man's face and reassessed the tall, broad-shouldered stranger, deciding three things right away: the man was tough, he wanted something in particular, and he'd be a hard one to put down in a fight. *But my fighting days are over*, Charlie told himself. *Unless I find the person who took my girls...*

"Help you with something, Sir?" he asked politely, moving toward the stranger.

"Are you Charlie Strout?"

"Yessir, that's me, what can I do for you today?" He raised both eyebrows. Getting a closer look at the man, Charlie could see that he was no dandy; that long scar running down his left cheek had obviously come from a knife and his nose appeared to have been broken at least once. He looked to be in his forties or so, but they'd clearly not been easy years.

The man stuck out his hand. "James O'Rourke. You wrote me a letter asking me to help you find your girls."

Charlie smiled widely and shook his hand vigorously. "Mr. O'Rourke, thank you so much for coming! I'd about given up on seeing you!" He shook his head sadly. "Seems like nobody wants to take on a case when the local authorities don't take it seriously..." Charlie grunted as he said the word 'authorities' in a most disrespectful manner.

"Can we talk somewhere?" Lucky asked, looking around.

"You bet, come with me," Charlie said, taking off his apron and heading toward the back of the large, cavernous building. "Freddy, you take over!" he yelled to a skinny, red-headed young man working nearby.

Freddy nodded and moved toward the front of the store, his big eyes taking in the rough-looking gentleman walking with his boss. *This can't be good*, he thought, shaking his head.

After seating Lucky comfortably on an old chair in the back room, Charlie poured his visitor and himself some coffee. "I asked around and your name kept coming up. Are you from Norfolk, Mr. O'Rourke?" he asked, leaning back in his own chair.

Lucky lifted his cup, took a long swallow of the strong, lukewarm brew and then set it back down on the barrelhead that they were using as a table. "No, Mr. Strout, I came to the area a year and a half ago to set up my own detective business. I started out as a policeman for ten years in Baltimore, and then worked for the Pinkerton Detective Agency for fifteen years after that. That job took me all over the Eastern Seaboard, in fact all that traveling was one of the reasons that I quit to work for myself. It was time to settle down somewhere, and I like this part of the country."

"You a married man?"

Lucky sighed. Why did everyone always want to know his marital status? "Never could find a gal who wanted to put up with the kind of work I do," he answered, leaving out a lot of pertinent details in that regard that he hoped nobody would ever find out about him.

Charlie nodded. "The women, they do like things to be settled down, that's for sure..." he said, getting a faraway look on his face. "Nelda, my Missus is – was – quite happy here in 'Lizbeth City, at least until all this happened... Now she's hard put just to get out of bed in the mornings, she's so worried about our girls..." He hung his head.

Lucky cleared his throat. Emotional parents were always hard to deal with, so he decided to get the conversation back on a more factual basis quickly. "So tell me exactly what happened, as far as you know, please, Mr. Strout."

"Call me Charlie, please."

"Alright, and you call me Lucky."

Charlie got a half-grin on his face and raised his eyebrows. *"Lucky?"*

Lucky rolled his eyes and sighed. "James William O'Rourke, actually – my mother was English and my father straight from Ireland. By the time I was six, I'd been in so many scrapes and close calls and come out unharmed that my Pa started calling me 'Lucky' and it sort of stuck. And I *have* been fairly lucky in my life – with a few exceptions," he added, absentmindedly running his forefinger over the scar on his cheek.

Charlie nodded, hoping that this nickname was a good sign that he'd chosen the right man for this job. He looked out the small window in the room toward the back alley. "Well, telling you all the details, that's part of the problem, Lucky – there's not much to tell. We went to bed one night, all of us safely tucked in, and got up the next morning and the girls were gone." He looked back at the other man, a heavy sadness in his eyes. "That was more than six weeks ago and we ain't seen them since..."

"Had they slept in their beds?"

"Looked like it."

"The girls' bedroom on the ground floor or second floor?"

"All our rooms are on the ground floor, except for the large attic, and nobody sleeps up there."

"Window left open?"

"It was an unusually warm night for early October; all our windows were open for any breeze we might get. It's hot and sticky here sometimes, you know." Charlie gave him a 'where-you-from-anyway, boy?' look.

Lucky ignored the jab and kept asking questions. "Had they been having any trouble with any of their friends, girls or boys?"

Charlie shook his head, looking straight into Lucky's eyes. "Nope. These are the same questions the Sheriff asked me, and I'm giving you the same answers. They were good girls who never gave us any trouble at all. We've got four kids; the other two are boys but are a good bit younger. Our boys, the other kids around here – they've all been questioned by us and by the Sheriff, but none of 'em knows nothing. I'm fairly confident that they're telling the truth, too. It's like the girls just vanished one night right out from under us, out of our own house..." He scrunched up his round face. "A person believes that they're safe in their own home, you know..."

"Well, Charlie, in a case like this sometimes it's the details that make the difference, so a person has to know where to look and what questions to ask. Don't give up. I'll look into it and we may turn up something that nobody else has even thought about and get your girls home." He tried to give the man an encouraging smile, but there really wasn't much of anything about this case to be encouraged about.

They visited together for another hour, Lucky getting all the details about the girls' lives, their friends, what they liked to do, and any other aspect of the case he could think of. Finally, he stood up and said, "Charlie, leave it to me now. I can't make you any promises, you know that, but I will tell you this: I'll do my dead-level best to find your girls. And I've had a lot of experience with cases like this, a lot more than your Sheriff. So, don't give up hope."

Charlie stood and extended his hand. "Thank you for coming, Lucky. You'd be welcome to stay in our home while you're here..."

As he took Charlie's hand, Lucky shook his head. "I appreciate the offer, but I don't want to be coming and going at all times of the day and night, disturbing your wife, for she's already got a lot on her. I'll take a room at the hotel and that'll be best for all of us."

"If you say so... the Southern Hotel, a few blocks down that way, is a right nice place. The Virginia Dare Hotel over on McMorrine St is lots newer, just depends on what you're lookin' for..."

"Which one is closest to the docks?"

Charlie shrugged. "It's a stone's throw down to Water Street from either one of 'em."

"Then I'll be staying at the Southern Hotel. You can find me there if you need me or to get a message to me. I'll come round and keep you updated on whatever information I get. You might not see me for a few days, but that's okay, it just means I'm out checking up on leads. How does that sound to you, Charlie?"

"Lucky, I do believe that for the first time since all this happened, you have given me some hope. Thank you for that!" He reached out and shook Lucky's hand vigorously.

Trying to be encouraging, Lucky smiled and nodded. But in all his experience, this did not sound like a case that held out a lot of hope. But he was determined to do his best to help the Strouts get their girls home.

Chapter 18

Lucky found the hotel and checked in. The Southern Hotel's black and white tile floor leading over to the Grand Staircase seemed a fitting analogy to Lucky when he saw it. This case was indeed black or white – the girls were either alive or they were dead. One outcome dark and final, one offering a bright hope that they would somehow be okay and come back to their parents.

After settling in, Lucky got himself organized and took a walk. Elizabeth City was a port town, located at a narrowed bend in the Pasquotank River. It was an old town that boasted of a lively history back into the mid-1700's. An early trading site, the tall-masted sailing ships brought trade here both to and from the new world early on. Before long, inspection stations, ferries, and all the accoutrements of civilization followed.

Lucky had been told that, with the construction and expansion of the Dismal Swamp Canal, most of the trading in the northeast Albemarle area made its way through Elizabeth City. It was known as a most hospitable harbor, both for its prime location and its friendly people.

Strolling down Main Street to Water Street, he began to get the feel of the place. Like most port towns, everything radiated out from where the ships docked, the center of life, business and activity.

After dinner at the hotel, Lucky took another walk, this time down by the docks, where no doubt most of the nefarious characters hung out and the area's questionable activity took place. That was true in any port town, and Elizabeth City should be no different.

Making himself comfortable on a stool at the bar in a local tavern, Lucky ordered a beer, about the only legal thing a tavern could sell since Prohibition. Then he struck up a conversation with a pretty barmaid. She was friendly, but not forthcoming with anything other than just the facts in answer to his questions about the people around the area.

After a few minutes of his questions, she stopped wiping the bar top, locked her beautiful blue eyes onto him, and said, "We get a lot of strangers in this place, people coming and going all the time. But you're not the usual run-of-the-mill fisherman, businessman or laborer. Why exactly *are* you here?" Her wide eyes studied him for a response.

"I *am* here on business," Lucky said, "but it's not your... *usual* business, you're right about that. I'm here..." he looked around, sizing up the privacy situation and lowered his voice, "to investigate the disappearance of the two Strout girls. Can you keep a secret?" He assumed that telling a barmaid this and asking her to keep quiet about it would be a sure-fire way for everybody in town to find out what he was doing here and thus come straight to him with any information they might have.

She looked him up and down and then put out her hand. "Helen's my name. What's yours?"

"Lucky O'Rourke," he said, shaking her outstretched hand. She smiled at him and he felt a little charge as he touched her; she was an unusual woman, he could tell that right away.

"Nice to meet you, '*Lucky*'," she said with a laugh, but then her look turned serious. "And I do hope you get lucky with this case – it's been weighing on everybody's mind around these parts. And yes, I can and will keep your secret."

Lucky couldn't help smiling at the girl. Well, she wasn't exactly a girl anymore, he judged her to be in her mid to late thirties, if he was any kind of expert at sizing up women – and he usually was. Her dark brown hair and those striking blue eyes, together with her ivory complexion, made her the kind of woman whose overall appearance grabs your attention, and then when you study her up close, you realize just how beautiful she actually is. *Why was she working at a bar? Why wasn't she married and settled down with a bunch of kids and some grateful man?* He had to wonder...

Lucky cleared his throat. "Yes, well, there's not much to go on, but sometimes having a fresh set of eyes looking at a problem can help."

She leaned forward and whispered, her nearness and the smell of her hair disconcerting him. "The Sheriff's not going to like what you're doing, I can tell you that right now! He's the kind of man that nobody crosses or questions and then lives to tell about it, if you take my meaning..." She shifted her eyes around the room to make sure that nobody was paying close attention to their conversation.

In order to be able to think, Lucky leaned back from the scent of Helen cleared his throat again and said, "Uh, yes, I have been told that... When the owner of this tavern comes in, would you direct me to him, please? Between you and him, I'm sure that you know most of what goes on around this town, the good and the bad."

She crossed her arms. "You're looking at the owner. *This is my place*," she said simply, tilting her head and staring him down as if she dared him to comment.

"Oh. Oh, sorry, I didn't mean..." he stammered.

She held up her hand to stop him. "It's okay, nobody expects a woman to own a tavern, but I do and that's that. There's a long story behind it and I might tell you about it someday if I get to know you better. But as for now, I close things down here around midnight or a little after. If you want to come back and talk then, I can spend a little time with you, but right now I'm too busy. I'm the only one working tonight."

"That's very kind of you, Helen. I'll take you up on that," he said, finishing his beer and standing up. "Till later, then," he said, throwing down the money for his beer together with a generous tip. He put his hat on, touched the brim to salute her, smiled and turned to leave. But he couldn't help noticing the look on her face as he did so –

amused, and perhaps a little… interested…? He whistled as he strode toward the door.

Poor schmuck, she thought, shaking her head as he walked out. *Thinks he'll come in here from the big city knowing nobody and actually solve this case…*

Two hours later he tapped on the door to the tavern. The shade on the door was down and she was now obviously closed for the night. Helen nudged the shade aside with her finger to see who was knocking and then unlocked the door and let Lucky in, locking up behind him. She directed him to a table.

"Have a drink?" she asked.

"If you will…"

"Well…" she said, looking him over. "Just one. Would a whiskey do for you?"

"Fine and dandy!" He wasn't about to ask where she got the illegal stuff.

After settling in, he exhaled heavily and began his pitch. "Thanks for taking the time to talk to me, I know you're busy. Look, Helen, I'm not trying to get anybody into trouble here, I'm just trying to find out what happened to those two girls. Their mother and father are beside themselves with worry. Anything you can tell me about, well, *anything* will help, I'm sure."

"First, you tell *me* a little about yourself, Lucky."

He thought for a moment. "What would you like to know?"

"Well, to start with – how'd you get into this line of work?" She lowered her chin and looked up at him.

"Hmmm.... Actually, I started out as a cop in Baltimore. No, wait, before that I was a young *petty-criminal* in Baltimore until a cop named Peters took me aside and had a long talk with me. He hauled me inside the police station and showed me the jail and the kind of people who were in there. Then he offered to help me do better for myself if I had a mind to... so I did, and became a cop myself."

She nodded. He considered that his signal to go on.

"After working as a cop for ten years in Baltimore, I got a job offer from the Pinkerton Detective Agency, and it looked interesting. So for fifteen years, up til last summer, I worked for them. That job took me all over the East from Massachusetts to Florida. I enjoyed the work but got tired of them telling me where to go and what to do, so I set myself up in business in Norfolk." He smiled and shrugged.

"You sound qualified, that's good. But what do you know about a place like Elizabeth City and what happens around these parts?" She challenged him with one perfectly arched black eyebrow.

He had to pull his attention away from those beautiful blue eyes. "People are people everywhere, Helen. There's good ones and bad ones, innocent ones and desperate ones. They do what they think they have to do, and that's something that the last twenty-five years has taught me holds true *no matter where* you are. I understand people and I'm good at my job." He gave her a *'well?'* look.

Helen took a sip of her drink and looked out into space, then returned her attention to Lucky. "So, you're not trying to hang anyone in particular with this or make some quick cash off the Strout's misfortune – you're truly looking into it with an open mind for the parents' sake?"

"Absolutely! I would normally assume that the girls have run away, but these circumstances are just too... odd ... for me to believe that. What do *you* think happened to them?" He tossed the ball into her court.

She looked down into her glass for a long moment and then lifted her long black lashes to stare him straight in the face. "I think something bad has happened to them."

He tilted his head; she seemed so sure about it. "Why?"

"Because they were good girls. I know them, I know their family; they've been raised right, I can tell you that. There are girls and then there are girls, if you know what I mean. These two are innocent, that much I'm sure of! They're not too far beyond the playing-with-dolls stage. But they were pretty, and you know how men are. Girls that young are gullible and believe everything that a man tells them."

Lucky could tell by the way she said it that Helen was far beyond believing everything any man told her. "So you think...?" he began.

She held up her hand. "I really don't know. All I can do is speculate. But there are a lot of men who do illegal things around here, as you probably know." She looked at his glass. "Where do you think that whiskey you're drinking came from?"

He blinked. "Well, since Prohibition, I'm pretty sure that it's either illegally imported or made somewhere locally?"

She nodded. "Have you ever heard of Buffalo City or East Lake Moonshine?"

He thought about it. "Yes, I believe I have..."

"Well, the stuff's made down in Buffalo City, across the Sound from here down past Manteo in the low country. Some kind of logging town, I think, I've never really been there. But the folks there make such fine moonshine that everywhere up and down the East Coast people are asking for it by name... and they won't take anything else because they know East Lake Moonshine by its golden amber color and its smooth taste!"

He picked up his glass, swirling the contents around and appreciating just how good this whiskey was. "What would that have to do with these missing girls?" He looked at her, obviously confused.

She sat up straight and took a deep breath, expelling it loudly. "Lucky, men from Buffalo City unload that stuff day and night here. And other men from all around load it up and take it and sell it. It's shipped from here to places – well, let's just say, all over the place!" she said, making a sweeping motion with her hand. "So we've got men coming and going all the time down by the docks. They're the kind of men who don't mind breaking the law, especially if they get to drinkin' their own moonshine. So then, if the girls ran into any of them..." She slumped a little and got a troubled look on her face.

He scrunched his eyebrows together. "But what would two good girls be doing alone down by the docks at night?"

She smiled at him. "Curiosity, probably. After all, they were pretty girls that got noticed everywhere they went, so maybe they decided to sneak out one night..." She looked at him and shrugged sadly.

He thought about what she'd said. "So you think that maybe some men from Buffalo City..."

"I don't know! Look, there are men here from all over the place! All I'm saying is that *if* these girls somehow wound up down by the docks late at night, something bad could have happened to them. I've given it a lot of thought, and that's about all I can come up with. Now, they may turn up, but you would think that by now, well, I just don't know..." She looked down and he could see her fighting the tears.

Lucky tilted his head and looked at Helen. She was a worldly wise woman for sure, but had her imagination run away with her on this? No doubt she knew the area and the people well. He needed to think about this, to visualize all the scenarios before he could buy into her theory; so he had some investigating to do.

He finished his drink in one long swallow, appreciating again the taste of East Lake Moonshine. "Helen, thanks for the drink – I'm gonna think about what you said. Of course, I have to investigate every possibility, but you know this town a lot better than me, so I'll be taking your opinion into consideration. I do appreciate you taking the time to talk to me."

She shook her head in a distracted manner, her long dark hair falling carelessly across her shoulders. "I'm only trying to help you, Lucky, and I hope to God that I'm wrong! Maybe those girls just ran off and got married and will turn up back here next week. That would be wonderful!" She tried to smile, but the effort never made it onto her face.

He smiled at her and, without thinking, reached across the table to take her hand. Then he looked into her eyes and said, "Helen, I wish everybody was as concerned about their neighbors as you are. You're a very special woman, you know that?" *Now, where did that come from*, he asked himself, feeling her soft hand in his.

She shook her head again, this time vigorously. "I'm nobody special, Lucky. It's just that I do worry about these people around here…" She looked up and he squeezed her hand.

"Thanks, Helen. You've been a big help."

She smiled at him in a way that made him feel warm all over. He'd thought those days were long past for him.

Chapter 19

Late the following morning, Lucky went down to hang around by the docks. The usual morning crowd, mostly fishermen, were already unloading their catch and haggling with the buyers. They must have been out since before daylight to be bringing in this much, this early. Lucky simply observed for a while, picking out the friendliest, most talkative of the lot and deciding his approach. After the buyers left and the men had set about cleaning their boats and getting ready for the next day's work, he wandered over toward one large man with a bulbous red nose and a hearty laugh.

"How was today's catch?" Lucky asked, looking around the boat.

The man saw him, pushed back his cap a bit and sized up this stranger. He grinned and said, "Let's just say that I've had a few hauls better and a whole lot more that were worse!" Laughing at his own joke, the man stuck out his dirty hand. "Zedikiah Freeman, call me Zed."

Lucky shook his hand and answered the man's broad smile with one of his own. "Lucky O'Rourke. Nice to meet you, Zed."

"I noticed ya hanging around here and watchin' us all," Zed said, hands on his hips. "If you're lookin' for illegal activity, you come at the wrong time of day. You some kind of law man?" he asked, obviously wary. "Cause if you are, I ain't got nuthin' to say nor nuthin' to hide, I stay on the straight and narrow. Cain't speak for all the fishermen of course," he added, grinning, "but most of us are just workin' hard to feed our families."

Lucky shook his head. "Nope. I'm no kind of law and that's the truth." He looked around cautiously and then said in a lowered voice, "Zed, I'm here looking into the disappearance of those two young girls. Their father has hired me because nobody has been able to turn up anything that might tell us what happened to them..."

Zed motioned for him to come up on the boat and take a seat. He sat too, took a handkerchief out of his pocket, mopped his brow and shook his head. "Bad business, that! Charlie Strout's a fine man and his family is church-goin' and all. This whole thing's been the subject of a lot of talk down here around the docks, but nobody seems to know nuthin'. Four of my six young'uns are girls, and I can tell you that if anything bad happened to any one of them, I'd be hell-bent on finding 'em myself, so I can understand Charlie bringing you in to help."

"Anybody putting forth any theories about what could have happened to them?" Lucky asked.

Zed thought about it. "Yeah, lots of theories, but don't none of 'em make sense, really. Fact is, the girls just disappeared." He stared at Lucky. "And that don't happen to two girls at once unless somebody does somethin'. So either the girls run off, which I don't really believe, or somebody took 'em off!"

"What about them getting lost in the woods or running into a wild animal?" Lucky ventured.

Zed harrumphed. "Nobody with any sense – even young'uns- would ever go into the deep woods 'round here at night! And what would be the chances of both of 'em say, falling into the water and drownin', you might ask?" He shook his head. "Kids round here learn to swim right after they learn to walk! No bodies have turned up, no sign of 'em anywhere... nope, I believe somethin' bad's happened to them girls, and if I was you, I'd be lookin' round the docks, but a lot later in the day, if you take my meaning..." He gave Lucky a raised-eyebrow look.

"Have you seen the kind of person hangin' round these parts who'd take off two young girls, Zed?"

Zed stared at him blankly. "What kind of person you mean? Men, rough men? You better believe it! If I found out any one of my girls had come down here after dark, I'd take a switch to their hiney so's they couldn't sit down for a week, and they'd never again think of doing anything that stupid!"

"Don't you think Charlie Strout would have warned his girls?"

Zed leaned back and made a face. "Yeah, but Charlie's a good man and he don't always see just how bad people can be," he answered, shaking his head sadly. "If he'd seen some of the things I seen around here... well, ain't no use blamin' him, I reckon, 'cause he'd a'never permitted it if he'd a'knowed. But I've raised some teenagers myself, and it only takes one to put the idea into the head of the others, and off they go!" He waved his big hand around.

Lucky studied the man. Obviously honest and caring, he was a straight talker, so he kept at him. "Zed, can I ask you about the Sheriff?"

Zed leaned back quickly, crossed his arms and sat up straighter. "What about him?"

"Do you think that he's an honest man – that he's really tried his best to find these girls? I'm asking because Charlie seems to have some doubts on that score..."

Uncrossing his arms and leaning back against the side of the boat, Zed studied Lucky for a long moment. He looked around casually to make sure that no one was eavesdropping on their conversation and then leaned forward, hands on his knees. "Sheriff Amos Graham is a dirty, low down, money-grabbin' fool! He looks the other way whenever anybody hands him some money, and then makes like he's earnin' his pay by botherin' honest folks just tryin' to make a livin'! All the moonshine that passes through this place – and there's a ton of it, mind you – every bit of it makes him a little more money that he stashes away somewhere. Why do you think it all goes through *here*?"

"So, are you saying that he'd look the other way on – *kidnapping or murder*?"

Zed shook his head. "I don't know, to tell you the truth. If it was one of his cronies that did it, he might just.

But it's more likely he probably don't care enough to do a good job of findin' out what happened. No money to be made there!" Zed got a disgusted look on his face.

Lucky nodded. "Thanks for your honesty, Zed, there aren't many folks who would come down on the side of truth like that, especially to a stranger."

"Well, I want you to find those girls – or at least what happened to them – for Charlie's sake. It's a terrible weight on a man, worrying about your young'uns. You got any yourself?"

Lucky shook his head. "No, my life's been too crazy to start a family so far..."

Zed grinned. "All it takes is the right gal, and things get straightened out pretty fast, let me tell you! I wasn't gonna get hitched myself until I had my own boat, but then I met my Ethel, and well..." he shrugged, "plans changed!"

Lucky laughed. "That's what people tell me; I guess I'll find out sooner or later myself."

"Sooner rather than later if you really are 'lucky', Lucky!" Zed grinned and winked at him.

Lucky shook hands and took his leave of the friendly fisherman. After talking to three more men, he got the same general sense of what they believed might have happened. And it all fell right into line with the beautiful Helen's line of thought. She was a wise woman, indeed.

Late that night Lucky wandered down to the docks, dressed in dark clothing and keeping to the shadows. He lurked around for hours studying the patterns of activity. One of the fishermen this morning had pointed in the direction of the sunset, telling him that there were some more docks down that way, secluded and used only at night. So for the next five nights, he went to various locations and simply observed the goings-on. In his spare time, he talked to everyone who was willing.

He could see that there was indeed a lot of moonshine coming and going from this place! Loads and loads would make it onto land, only to be stacked back up onto wagons or different boats later that same night. The rattle of the glass bottles as they were tossed around would be so loud that Lucky was surprised none of them broke outright and spilled white lightning all over the place.

Most of the men were fairly businesslike about it, but now and then a few would obviously be under the influence of their product and make so much noise that the Sheriff would have had to be deaf not to hear it if he even half-tried. Some of the men from the boats would occasionally wander into town, seeking out the places that stayed open early into the morning hours to provide amusement for that particular group of customers. But wandering around those places asking questions could get a fella hurt bad or killed... and Lucky had the scars to prove it.

He had a lot of experience staying in the background and tailing people, so he wasn't spotted, even by these cautious men.   Besides, this group obviously felt fairly safe in Elizabeth City under this particular Sheriff's 'protection.' The one thing that kept popping up was the mention of Buffalo City and the "East Lake" label on the jugs of moonshine; seems like most of it did indeed come from down that way.

This seemed to Lucky like a good time to make a trip into the lowcountry to visit this place called Buffalo City.

Chapter 20

Lucky managed to buy himself a ride the next morning on the *Hattie Creef*, a boat filled with supplies headed for Buffalo City. He tried to start up conversations with the men who worked on that boat. Obviously wary, they gave him little to no real information.

Yes, they admitted that a lot of moonshine made its way out of the town, but *no*, they didn't know of anyone in particular who was making or selling it. One crusty old man told him flat-out that what the people in Buffalo City did was their own business, and looking directly at him added, "And it ain't none of your'n, neither, Mister!"

Sitting quietly on a box of supplies, Lucky studied the water as they made their way south. The Albemarle Sound was large, but all in all it wasn't fearsome water and looked to be the kind of run that could be made easily and on a regular basis. As he was contemplating how best to approach these isolated people to get information, the captain came over and sat down beside him, offering him a drink out of a canteen. Lucky smiled and took a swig, recognizing it instantly as the smooth Buffalo City moonshine.

The captain stared out into the water and spoke, "Well, as I see it, Mister, you ain't no lawman, 'cause all them Revenooers and Coast Guard types got their own boats and never beg rides on mine. You don't look like a businessman, neither. So what in the world are you doing headed to that gator-ridden little village for, anyway?" He turned to look directly at Lucky. "I mean, *the truth*, you understand!" He gave Lucky the kind of look that told him that if he didn't tell the truth he might never arrive at his destination.

Lucky nodded. "You heard about those two girls that disappeared from Elizabeth City?"

The captain nodded slowly. "Bad business, that..."

"Sure is. Well, the father of those girls has hired me to try to find out what happened to them. It's as simple as that." He gave a wide-eyed look to the sailor and tilted his head.

"Captain Wes Holman," the big man said, extending his rough hand.

"Lucky O'Rourke. Nice to meet you." They shook hands and Lucky waited to see if the man would volunteer any information, because he certainly looked like the type who wouldn't be questioned.

After a long minute the captain took a deep breath and said, "Well, how's it goin' so far? You finding out anything?"

Lucky shook his head. "Not much, really... I'm headed down to Buffalo City to see if I can make any connection between the moonshine runners and the girls, but it's a stretch..."

Holman turned and looked at him. "You ain't gonna just git off the boat and start askin' if anybody down there is a murderer or a kidnapper, are you?"

Lucky laughed. "No, Captain, I find that generally if I want to get into a place it's better if I sneak around to the back door or go in a side window rather than crashing in through the front door ..."

Holman nodded. "Smart. Those people are cut off from the rest of the world, except for what lumber goes out of there, and these days there ain't much of that. But they're not stupid, either. They're a tight knit community, and they look after each other. Because of the moonshine, any strangers that show up are automatically considered as dangerous outsiders..."

"You have any helpful advice for me, Captain?"

"Hmmm.... Well, from what I see, the place is fairly equally divided between whites, colored people and Russians, although the groups don't mix with each other much. So, if I was you, I'd speak to the white folks first because they love to talk the best of all of 'em and generally know what's going on. The colored people look at you suspiciously and the Russians pretty much keep to themselves when it comes to outsiders."

He spat overboard and wiped his mouth with a dirty handkerchief pulled from his pocket. "But a few of the Russians that are still there are bad business and they don't mind hurtin' a person if need be. I've seen some of 'em tear into strangers, so don't mess with *them* unless you have to..."

Lucky nodded. "Thanks, Captain; that's all good to know and I'm sure that it will come in handy. And I'd appreciate your keeping it under your hat who I am and what I'm doing..."

Captain Holman nodded once. "Done."

They sat companionably in silence for several minutes. "We'll be back in three days' time if'n you need a ride back to EC," Homan said. "For what it's worth and as bad as I hate to admit it, I think you might be onto something here, and I wish you the best of luck in findin' out what happened to those girls." He shook his head. "I got a couple of girls myself, and I don't think I could rest neither if they just up and disappeared!"

With that the Captain stood up, nodded, and took himself off toward the wheelhouse, leaving Lucky to ponder how many men had told him virtually the same thing about their own daughters.

As they pulled in to dock at Buffalo City, Lucky took the measure of the place as best he could from the boat. *Not much of a town*, he decided. The main street itself had a train track running right down the middle of it. *Odd.* There were some businesses, a hotel of sorts and a lot of people standing around looking toward the boat.

A few wagons pulled by mules were hitched up but empty. Although it looked as though the boat had been expected, nobody seemed to be in a hurry for anything; after they'd docked and everything was all tied down, some of the men eventually began sauntering toward the boat looking mildly interested.

Sizing up the situation, Lucky saw indeed that there was a mix of colored people, poor whites and (by their dress and speech) people of some foreign extraction; they were the Russians, he presumed. He helped the captain and his crew to unload the supplies, grabbed his bag and then headed for the hotel. He didn't stay to see what – if anything – was being loaded back onto the boat for the return trip.

The people he passed on the street eyed him suspiciously. At the hotel, he gave the lady his name as James Williams, his usual alias; the aging proprietress, Mrs. Needles, eyed him cautiously but gave him a room. She wanted to know how long he'd be there and what his business was in Buffalo City, so she didn't hesitate to ask.

"Well, Ma'am, I'm not sure how long I'll stay, no more than a few days to a week I expect, and as to my business in town..." he leaned forward, putting his hands flat on the countertop, "I'm here to check out the town because I'm thinking of moving here and starting up a business."

"What kind of business you talkin' bout?" she asked sharply, sensing competition for the little bit of money that came into town. The way Buffalo City had been headed downhill the past decade or so would naturally make her suspicious that anybody in their right mind would be coming here to start up anything.

Lucky had seen the many cases of empty glass jugs on the supply boat. "Oh, nothing that would compete with your lovely hotel here," he assured her, and saw her exhale a sign of relief. "Actually, Ma'am, I've got a little glassworks up in Richmond. I've been thinking of expanding and heard that ya'll might be in need of a glass maker. I'm thinking of setting up a little business making glass jugs, you know, the one-and-five-gallon sturdy types..." He raised both eyebrows.

She raised one eyebrow. "Are you some kind of lawman?"

"Heavens, no, Ma'am! I'm just a fella who sees a business opportunity and knows what to do with it! You think there might be a market here for a glassworks?"

"You'd be hiring some local men, then?" she responded noncommittally.

"Naturally. I'd need several good men who aren't afraid of a little hard work. First I'd have to build a large building to work in, but with all this lumber that would be easy enough; then the supply boats could haul in the rough materials I'll need. I suspect sand would be fairly easy to come by in these parts. I'd be bringing in my own crew to get set up and train everybody, and naturally, they'd be staying here at your hotel..."

A big smile appeared on her thin face. "Of course," she said, nodding. "Well that's fine and dandy! We're glad to have you in our little town, Mr. Williams, and if there's anything I can do to help you, well then you just let me know…"

"First off, I'd like to go to my room and unpack, get something to eat and then maybe take a walk around town, I think."

"Supper is at six o'clock, but I'll send up a tray with a little something to hold you til then," she said, smiling. "And before you go on your walk, I'll give you a little history of our town and all the people in it!"

After enjoying his light meal and an informative conversation with Mrs. Needles, Lucky strode out onto the wooden porch, looking both ways before deciding to head to the right. According to the hotel proprietress, this was the way down to the place where the logs were loaded from the water (when they had been floated into town) and from the railroad cars that brought them in from the deep woods. Much of it then went out by boat to be made into cypress shingles, boat lumber and other kinds of wood products. There was even a small pulp mill nearby.

No one was working there at the moment, but Lucky could easily picture the men hoisting the logs up out of the water by the large pulley system or swinging them over to the flatbed rail cars parked there to take them to the mill.

These men were hard workers, he'd give them that. Dragging those trees out of the swampy lowlands after having cut them down by hand, well, that alone would be backbreaking labor; not to mention the miserable working conditions in this hot swampy country full of bears, bobcats and alligators.

Mrs. Needles had mentioned that the men made fifty cents a day, and most of that was paid in company script, called *pluck*, which could only be spent at the local store or traded for other goods around town. Lucky shook his head sadly. *The things men had do to feed their families*, he thought. It took a special kind of desperation to do this kind of work in this kind of place, but then the country was in a depression all over, so people simply did what they had to do and were glad for any kind of work.

Moonshining, hard as it was, would be easy work compared to logging. But it was dangerous, illegal work done by serious businessmen, so he'd have to be careful not to stir up too much unwanted interest before leaving this place. He walked up and down the main street, noticing that the whole town was built on the north side of Mill Tail Creek. Evidently the cypress, juniper and pine that they harvested was of high quality; there was a big boat building industry all up and down the east coast that constantly needed a healthy supply of good lumber.

When he returned to the hotel for supper, he noticed that the dining room was filled with a few women and several men, all of whom eyed him but said nothing. A low murmur was all he could hear during his meal, which he ate while sitting alone. When he was finished, he got up, thanked the cook and walked outside to go sit out on the porch. He looked around at the other buildings, noticing their clapboard construction. All of them seemed to be a little defective, off-kilter; they had obviously been built of the rejects of the lumber mill. He smiled, realizing that nothing out here would be thrown away.

A few minutes later a couple of rough-looking characters made their way out onto the porch and took a seat, one on each side of him.

"So, you're from Richmond, Mr. Williams?" one man asked warily.

Lucky smiled. Evidently Mrs. Needles had been fueling the rumor mill, and he suspected that by now everyone in town knew who he was and what he was here for.

"Yep. Thinkin' of setting up a glass factory in this nice little town of yours." Lucky said, smiling. "Are you men local businessmen yourselves?"

They shared a cautious look and then the second man stuck out his hand. "Josiah Knowles," he said. Lucky shook his hand.

The first man introduced himself. "Wilbur Bent." He shook Lucky's hand as well.

"If ya'll already know that my name is Williams, then you probably know what my business here in Buffalo City is, too?" Lucky asked.

Josiah Knowles laughed a throaty laugh. "Yeah, well, it's a small town, Mr. Williams, and we don't get too many visitors these days..."

Lucky smiled but decided that being the listener in this situation would be the best approach.

Wilbur Bent cleared his throat and asked, "What makes you think that our little town needs a glassworks, Mr. Williams? Kind of an odd business to set up way out here, don't you think?"

Lucky sorted the situation out quickly. Wilbur was the front man, but Josiah was the brains behind whatever was going on. So he turned to address Josiah. "Let me be honest with you two gentlemen," he said, using the term quite loosely. "All up and down the east coast, East Lake Moonshine is being requested at speakeasies and by individuals who don't particularly agree with Prohibition. Seems that people can't get enough of the stuff, and I figured that all of it goes out of here in jugs, so this might be a good market for my high quality glass." He shrugged. "But if I'm wrong, then I can go somewhere else to set up..." He stared blankly at them and waited.

Bent looked at Knowles and raised an eyebrow. Knowles nodded slightly and said, "Well, it's true that a lot of product goes out of here, Mr. Williams, but most of it is shipped in crockery jugs – they're sturdy, you know. And we get a pretty good price on the jugs we order out of Norfolk... you'd have to go some to beat that price..."

The man gets right down to business, Lucky thought. *No need messing around either, because they'll either believe me or kill me.* "I have a good source for my materials and it looks like there's no shortage of sand nor men that need work around here, so I expect that my prices would be very attractive. And yes, crockery is strong, but my glass is even stronger and weighs a lot less. That extra weight slows you down out in the water, you know."

Lucky stretched his long legs out and crossed his feet at the ankles, leaning back in his wooden straight chair, tipping it onto the two back legs. "But some towns don't take to strangers coming in, and if this is one of them, then I'll just be on my way back to Richmond and no offense taken. I'm in business to make money and if there's none to be made, then I'll leave ya'll alone and go on my way to set up somewhere else." He smiled at both of them in a most relaxed manner.

Josiah and Wilbur shared a look, then Knowles stood up and said, "Let me check around with some of the other businessmen in town, Mr. Williams, and we'll get back to you in a day or two. How does that sound?"

Lucky stood up and stuck out his hand. "Fair enough. And in the meantime, I'd like to talk to the townsfolk and get a sense of what living and working here would be like for my people. I'll look forward to hearing from you." He nodded his head as Knowles and then Bent shook hands with him.

The two men said their goodbyes and walked down the street, their heads together. Lucky knew that if he survived the night, he was 'in' and would get some information. He cleared his throat and headed to the local tavern, to get to know some more of the locals.

Chapter 21

After a couple of rounds at the local tavern and a lot of small talk with several locals, Lucky went back to his hotel room for the night. He locked the door and braced a chair under the knob. *For all the good it would do,* he told himself. But if these men didn't believe him and suspected that he was a lawman, he wasn't going to go down without a fight. He thought of Helen and how she'd said that this was dangerous business.

Between the corrupt sheriff and unscrupulous moonshiners, he was taking quite a risk investigating this case. But this wasn't his first rodeo, so he realized the danger involved. He put his pistol under his pillow and tried to get some sleep.

What seemed like mere moments later, he opened his eyes to see the sunlight streaming in through the dirty window. The chair was still lodged under the doorknob and there was no sign of anyone having tried to break in. Lucky laughed to himself. He'd been in this line of work so long that he could sleep even when his life was in danger!

After getting dressed, he went down and had a bite of breakfast. Mrs. Needles was all smiles to see him and asked how he'd slept.

"Like a baby," he replied, smiling. She seemed quite pleased with that response.

"So, you'll be with us for a while, then?" she asked.

He nodded. "I'll be scouting around town looking for property to build on and talking to people about what it's like to live here, Mrs. Needles. Do you think that people here will talk to me, me being a stranger and all?"

"Oh, I expect you'll find the folks in Buffalo City to be quite friendly," she said, grinning. Obviously, the word was out and the general consensus was that everybody was all for new money coming into town.

He left and walked down to the Dareforest General Store. A few men were sitting out on the porch in front, talking and laughing. They saw him coming and one of them waved in a friendly manner.

I wish I had a Mrs. Needles to lay the groundwork for me in every town I went to, he thought, waving back and smiling.

The three men on the porch offered him a seat and were quite happy to answer any question he had about the town. They informed him that it had once been the largest settlement in Dare County, but now they weren't sure, since the population had fallen off some and they themselves didn't get out much. But they assured him that the locals would welcome anybody who was bringing in work to the area.

He went inside and met Max Stanford, the extremely friendly storekeeper (who obviously was hoping to make a little money from the glass market on one end or another) and chatted amiably for a while with the man. Then he set off down toward the docks. A few fishermen here were hauling in their catch for the day, still trying to make an honest living in the place.

One of them, Booger Jenkins (Lucky didn't even want to think about how Booger had earned his nickname) was especially helpful. The old man had a small fire burning onshore and was roasting some of his catch; he invited Lucky to join him and have some, which he did.

Fresh fish, Lucky thought, picking the tender white flesh off the bones with his fingers, *nothing like it*, and he told Booger just how good it was.

Booger grinned and agreed wholeheartedly.

After a half hour of friendly chitchat, Lucky asked casually, "This town doesn't have too many rough characters in it, does it? I mean, my men will be bringing their families down when they come…"

"Oh, no," Booger said, but then added, "if you know who to stay away from, that is…"

Lucky raised an eyebrow. "Hmmmm…. I sure don't want to put any of my people in danger!"

Waving his dirty hand, Booger said, "Aww, it ain't nuthin, really, it's just that some of them Russians are a little crazy, 'specially when they been passin' round the fruit jar… One of 'em lately's been actin' like some kinda tough guy, since he got his own boat, and is pullin' in big money runnin' loads of… *well, you know*… And the Irish, when they git drunk can git a little crazy and hard to handle, too, 'specially that one that runs with the Russian, Sasha." He shook his head.

Lucky nodded. "Yes, Booger, I do know what those loads are, and that's exactly why I'm coming to Buffalo City to build my glassworks. The need for glass jugs here is growing all the time, I understand... and the future for my business looks good," he said, grinning.

Exhaling loudly, Booger said, "Yeah, I'd heard that you... that is to say, that you were... *well, you know...*"

"I believe that every man has a right to make a living the best way he can, and that includes me. I'll be providing a product to people who provide a product to other people who provide a little fun and relaxation," Lucky said, shrugging. "And I don't see a problem with that at all!"

Obviously impressed with Lucky's business acumen, Booger nodded and said, "Good to know we can trust you." We get strangers in here from time to time who pretend to be somebody they're not just to try to stop the bootleggin', but there ain't no stopping somethin' that people want as bad as they want the Buffalo City moonshine!"

Lucky nodded philosophically, shrugging his shoulders and extending his hands out palm-up. "So tell me more about the Russians..." he said, leaning forward.

Booger lit up and smiled big. "Well," he said, straightening up and cocking his head, "most of 'em are alright, a little peculiar about food and such and talkin' that spittin', growling-sound language of theirs, but for the most part they're harmless enough. But if you git one of 'em drunk or make him mad, then you'd best git outta their way or be ready to git beat stupid!

Lucky gave him a 'not really?' look.

"Yep. They're all that way when they git the hard stuff, but there's one of 'em – the one I told you about who's gittin' above himself lately – he can be like two different people, I swear. Sasha's his name – a big ole blonde feller who got his own boat more'n a year back and went from nuthin to somethin' real quick. When he's sober, he's as pleasant as the day is long, but when he gits mad or to bendin' the elbow at the tavern, he turns nasty – and I mean *nasty*!" He shook his head, made an ugly face and shivered.

"Like nasty enough to kill somebody?"

Without hesitating, Booger nodded. "I personally seen him beat one of the colored men – and I mean a great big one, mind you – nearly to death. Poor feller's still walkin' funny! And that other young feller he goes around with, his name is Ryan somethin-or-nother, he's just mean as a snake *all the time*; he's got a look about him that makes you wanna run the other way. Why, since Virgil left they can't seem to keep no help workin' on their boat; nobody wants to work with 'em for long! And I heard they pay good, so..." He clucked and shook his head.

Lucky raised an eyebrow. "Virgil? Who's Virgil?"

Booger was on a roll. "Yeah, nice enough kid whose daddy got killed at the mill some years back. He's a hard worker who takes care of his mamma. Well Virgil, he worked with the two of 'em for a long time. Then all of a sudden he picked up and left and moved to..." He looked around and scrunched up his sun-weathered face. "...Ocracoke, I think. He got married, moved off and left his Ma here. Word is that she wouldn't go with him, but I think that he just didn't want to take her; she's a mean ole...*well, you know*... woman." Booger looked a little embarrassed for thinking such thoughts about an old lady.

Lucky passed the time of day with Booger for another hour. Then he said his goodbyes and moved on down the street to talk to another gaggle of fellas who were just standing around – there seemed to be an endless supply of them in Buffalo City. It made him glad that he wasn't really opening up a business here; these men had gotten used to hanging out with each other, drinking and spinning yarns and might not like real work anymore.

After supper he took off down to the tavern again to visit with Walt Hollins, the bar owner. Beer was the legal drink of the day, but you had only to request 'something else' for the glass jug to come out from behind the counter. Lucky sat and listened to the talk around him. People would occasionally come by, slap him on the back and share a few words. It had not even been two days yet and already he was a very popular man in town.

He could pick out the Russians in the place easily enough by their heavy accents. After an hour or so, a big, loud blonde fellow walked in with a smaller, weasely-looking guy at his side; the two of them took a seat at one of the tables. Lucky noticed that most heads turned either away from or toward the Russian and his friend when they made their appearance, but nobody seemed to ignore them completely.

The barkeep quickly went over and took their order, and then promptly brought them both a large mug of beer. A few brave souls would wander over and share a word or two, but most of the other patrons either kept to themselves or decided that this might be a good time to leave.

Lucky smiled and nodded at the two men but didn't approach them. He kept sitting at the bar, talking with the owner about the town and business here. The bartender kept a close eye on the two men, warily watching to make sure that neither of them ran out of beer. After his third trip to their table, Walt shook his head and muttered, "Not tonight, please God!"

"Is there a problem, Mr. Hollins?" Lucky asked, curiously looking around.

"Don't look – *at them*!" Walt whispered.

Lucky tilted his head. "You mean the big blonde fellow and his friend?" he asked innocently, nodding his head in their direction.

Making sure that Sasha and Ryan were not paying attention, Walt leaned forward, wiping the bar top and saying in a low voice, "Those two are bad news, and a whole heap of trouble when they git drunk. They've busted up the place a few times lately and I just don't want to see it happen again tonight!"

"They look harmless enough…"

"Yeah, well, looks can be deceiving, Mr. Williams, and I advise you to stay away from both of 'em, and I mean far away. They've gotten beyond themselves with all the money they're making hauling 'shine and they're turning bad fast!" He shook his head. "And they ain't never been good boys! Well, Virgil was, but that Ryan is bad to the bone and always has been and the Russian, *huh*, he's just plain crazy! One minute he's fine like he's your best buddy, and then he turns on you like a mad dog! Now that he's got a little money he's more than bad – he's dangerous!" He looked into Lucky's eyes. "But you didn't hear that from me, you understand?"

Lucky nodded. "Of course, Walt. Who's this Virgil you mentioned? Somebody else was talking about him, and he sounds like a good man. Would he be available to work for me, do you think?"

"Nope, he moved off, and I say good for him! I wouldn't want to work with those two, either! His Ma is here and I heard he sends money to make sure she's alright, but he stays well away from them two," Walt said, nodding toward Sasha's table.

"Who's his Ma?"

"That would be Mrs. Timmons, she lives in the last red house on the west end of the road behind the store. She's a piece of work, that one. Nobody likes her, I don't know why she stays here... I suppose it's hard for older folk to move away from a place if they've lived there awhile. If it wasn't for her son, she'd probably starve to death, but I heard she refused to move to Ocracoke with him when he got married."

"What kind of work does Virgil do?"

"Well, he was in on the boat with Sasha and Ryan haulin' likker when they first started, and they was doing pretty good, but then all of a sudden, a couple of months ago, he up and left 'em. Found him a girl in Ocracoke and went to work for her father fishin' for a living, got married and settled down, I heard." He looked up, lifted his rag and stuck his finger out. "But he was a good man, Virgil was. Would help anybody out anytime you needed him. Hated to see him go..."

Lucky thanked the barkeep, tipped him generously and got up to go back to his room at the hotel. As he passed by their table, Sasha reached out and grabbed him by the wrist, clamping down hard and stopping him. Lucky's head spun around and their eyes met.

"Seet down, Stranger, and have a drink vid us," Sasha said in a friendly manner. "Ve vould like to get to know you." He released Lucky's wrist.

Lucky turned and faced them both with a big smile. "And I'd like nuthin' better myself, boyees, but I'm afraid I've had a little too much *(hiccup)* to drink and need to get back to the hoootel before I fall down," he said with a grin and a very unmanly giggle. "I got stufffft to do tomorrow, and a bad head won't help me do it! Maybe nesst time?" he asked, grinning stupidly.

Sasha laughed out loud. "Da, I know vat that is like, meester. I got me some work to do in the morning myself! Ve talk to you next time, da?"

Lucky grinned again and nodded, then turned and walked unsteadily toward the door. Sometimes the smartest defense was simple stupidity.

Chapter 22

The next morning after breakfast Lucky struck up a conversation with Mrs. Needles about Virgil Timmons. The coincidence that Virgil had up and left the Russian not long after the time of the girls' disappearance kept popping up in his mind, floating around and refusing to be pushed down, like a cork on a fishing line. And when that particular thing happened, Lucky had learned not to ignore it.

"… and I've heard from several people that Virgil's a fine young man. Do you think that he'd consider coming back to Buffalo City to work for me, Mrs. Needles?"

She shook her head. "Probably not, Mr. Williams. He's all married and settled in Ocracoke now and you know how it is with newlyweds…" She giggled a little and batted her eyelashes at him.

Lucky tried hard not to flinch. "Yes, Ma'am, I reckon I do," he said. "Too bad, though, because I'm looking for a man like Virgil to run the place for me after I get it all going…"

She nodded. "He was a good young man, took care of that shrew of a mother of his. Those three boys had themselves a real good…business," she said. "But then Virgil took off like a bullet and has hardly been seen since. I guess love'll do that to a person…"

"How did the boys get started in business?" Virgil asked casually.

Mrs. Needles thought about it for a long moment. "You know, I've asked myself that same question because they went from being poor boys who had nuthin' to three boys who had a boat in one day. I don't know personally where they got that boat – nobody seems to, but that was the very thing that pushed 'em up in the world, that's for sure!"

"Well, I'll be seeing you later, Mrs. Needles," Lucky said, tipping his hat. "I may be catching a ride back to Elizabeth City on the supply boat when it comes in this afternoon. I have to go home and do some serious figuring on how to set up this business, but it looks like Buffalo City is just the place I thought it would be, maybe even better! So I'll be returning soon to finalize some more details on acquiring land and such."

She patted her hands together. "Wonderful, Mr. Williams, wonderful! A breath of fresh air you'll be around here, too! You just let me know when you're comin' – we do have a post office here, and even a telegraph line, you know – and I'll get as many rooms ready as you need!"

"You're a jewel of the first order, Ma'am," he said, smiling. "And I wouldn't stay anywhere else." *Unless there were some other places to stay*, he thought.

Lucky walked down to the docks looking for Booger, who was proving to be a great source of information. When he saw him later that morning cleaning his boat, he walked up and shook his hand.

"My buddy Booger, how you doing, man?" he asked.

"Jes fine, Mr. Williams! Had a good catch today, too! Would you consider takin' a bite of fish with me?" He nodded toward the fire he'd started up over on the shore.

Lucky glanced over at the catch he'd brought in. "And get some of that good wahoo? You bet your biscuits I'd like that, and thank you for it!"

They sat together and ate a few fish, then Lucky pulled out a flask. "Let me return your kindness, have a drink, my friend!" he said, handing the flask to Booger, who took it without a second thought.

"Mighty gen'rous of you, Mr. Williams!"

"Booger, you must call me James, all my friends do!"

Booger grinned and took a long pull on the flask. "So, James, how's things goin' for you here in Buffalo City?"

"Well, it looks to be a finer place than I had imagined, to tell you the truth. I don't think I'll have any trouble finding good workers once I get going, but I have to say that I'm having a bit of a problem finding that one good man to run the works once it's all set up... I heard tell of a young man named Virgil Timmons who sounded like just what I was looking for, but they say he's up and left..." Lucky sighed and shrugged.

Taking another long pull on the flask, Booger nodded. "Yep. Virgil was a fine boy and a willin' worker; he helped me out a few times when he was younger. Even after he got hooked up with that crazy Russian he was still a good 'un. But you'll find somebody else, I'm sure. They's lotsa men needin' work. And I'm pretty sure Virgil ain't comin' back!"

Lucky chatted with Booger about boats for another fifteen minutes and then, after he figured that enough moonshine had passed those flapping lips to loosen them up, he asked, "So where did those boys – I mean Virgil and the Russian – get that boat of theirs to begin with?"

Booger sat up and made an expression on his face that almost made Lucky laugh; he was thinking hard, and it showed. He pointed his finger at Lucky's face.

"You know, we all of us wondered about that very thing! One day they were just three poor boys, and the next day they had themselves a boat. It was a hunka junk, mind you, but it was runnin'. They put money into it and now it's sailin' across the sound, though it still don't look like much..."

Lucky looked up and to the left, rubbing his chin. "Hmmm...Now, that is peculiar. Where would three poor boys get themselves a boat like that?"

Booger shrugged. "Don't know. Nobody seems to know. I heard somethin' about them winnin' it in a poker game, but I couldn't rightly believe that..." He took another swig.

"Anybody round these parts missing a boat, or anybody turn up looking for one?" Lucky ventured.

Booger was doing some more heavy thinking by the look on his face. Suddenly he sat up straight. "You think they coulda – *stole it*?" He looked shocked. "There's some things a man don't do, James, and stealin' another man's boat is one of 'em!"

Lucky shook his head. "Oh, no, I wouldn't accuse anybody of that, but... it does seem odd that one day they don't have it and the next day they do..." He shrugged.

Booger was disturbed. Among watermen, their boats were sacrosanct. Stealing a boat would be an unforgiveable sin. After a while he said, "Well, nobody turned up lookin' for one or accusin' anybody, so I don't reckon it was nuthin like that... but I wouldn't put it past the Russian, that's for sure!" A look of puzzlement and confusion stayed on his face despite his denial of a heinous crime like boat thievery happening in Buffalo City...

Lucky said his goodbyes, left Booger scratching his head and muttering and walked back to the hotel to pack. The pieces of the mystery were still floating around unattached, but it looked like some of them were beginning to be drawn together. The truth was a powerful thing and would not be kept down; Lucky had learned that long ago.

Chapter 23

"I'll be in touch with you soon, Mrs. Needles," Lucky said, paying her in cash for his room and board for the two nights and three days.

She smiled. "Your're welcome anytime and we look forward to seeing you again, Mr. Williams," she answered, fingering the cash fondly before putting it into the drawer.

"I've never met your husband, is Mr. Needles well?" he asked.

She fluttered her eyelashes at him. "My dear Mr. Needles died of a fever these two years past, and I've been doing my best to keep the hotel in business without him..." She tried without success to put on the look of a helpless Southern belle.

Lucky was sure that even if there ever had been a Mr. Needles, that she'd been the one keeping this place running long before he had passed away. And he also suspected that Mr. Needles might have taken a fever just to get away from his wife.

"I'm so sorry, dear lady," he said, reaching across the counter and patting her hand. "But you're doing a fine job of it, I must say. I look forward to my return." He smiled his most charming smile.

"Will you be bringing Mrs. Williams with you?" she asked casually.

He shook his head. "I'm a bachelor, Mrs. Needles, so I'll just be needing the single room if you please."

She smiled widely, her worn face revealing a few missing teeth. "I'll be looking forward to seeing you myself, Mr. Williams." She turned her hand over and squeezed his. "You'll find that we will provide you with a *warm* welcome when you return."

Lucky walked down to the docks and waited for the supply boat. *Anything to get out of the hotel lobby*, he thought. Within the hour, Captain Holman and his crew steamed up Mill Tail Creek and pulled alongside the dock. He waved and boarded the boat after they'd secured everything.

"Give me a lift back to Elizabeth City, Captain?" Lucky asked.

Captain Holman smiled. "Glad to see you again, Lucky! And happy to give you a lift! But we'll be going south to Ocracoke this evening after we unload here; it's our monthly trip down there. We'll be putting to there for the night, and then back to Elizabeth City in the morning. Would that do for you?"

Lucky smiled. He was living up to his nickname once again. "That will be just fine, Captain, as I've been wanting to visit that little island!"

The sun was beginning to set over the Croatan Sound, and Lucky could not have imagined a more beautiful sunset over the water. When the boat pulled up to the dock on Silver Lake at Ocracoke, Lucky was immediately taken with the place. Homes and businesses were nestled around the 'lake', a natural bay that provided docks and safe harbor for all kinds of vessels. He could hear a fiddler playing a tune somewhere as they floated in across the water.

"You can sleep out on the deck if you want," Captain Holman told him after they'd secured the boat. "There's a hotel out on the point, the Cedar Grove Inn, you can walk it. Or there's some places that rent rooms, I understand," he said, nodding toward the shore. "Most of us will be going over to the Jolly Roger for a bite and a pint," he added, nodding toward the shore where several lanterns were hung around a place that was apparently the source of the fiddle music. "You're more than welcome to join us..."

Lucky did just that and found himself eating a delicious meal with the captain and his crew at a large table with long benches overlooking the water. Dark had fully descended now and the light from the lanterns danced on the water. A pretty young barmaid was serving their food and drink. She smiled at him shyly. He returned her smile and tried to find the right moment to approach her. After a while, he noticed her standing at the bar cleaning glasses and wandered over.

"Hello, Miss," he said, using his most charming voice and smile. "My name is James and I'm new here..."

She looked at him skeptically and said, "Are you just passing through?"

He nodded. "And I'm thinking of taking a room for the night. Do you have any suggestions?"

She looked him over. "Well, there's the Cedar Grove Inn and the Pamlico Hotel. But my Ma rents rooms. Just for the one night, you say?"

He nodded again. "I'm a businessman and will be going back to Elizabeth City tomorrow. I just need a bed and some place to wash up."

"Well, then," she said, looking satisfied, "I'll give you directions to my ma's place. It's on this side of the creek and just a street over there," she said, nodding toward town. You can walk it, no problem."

"I'll get my bag and make my way over there now, if it's alright. I'm not a man who keeps late hours and I just want to get a good night's sleep."

She nodded, smiled at him and gave him the directions he needed.

He talked with Captain Holman and made arrangements to get back to the boat tomorrow before they took off mid-morning.

As he walked toward the boarding house, Lucky felt an unusual sense of peace come over him. Glancing around, he noticed the soft lantern light coming from inside the houses and heard the trickle of conversation from all the porch-sitters scattered around. *There's something about this place*, he thought, *that makes you want to slow down. That makes you feel like time itself has slowed down...*

When he reached the house, he knocked on the door, introduced himself and was welcomed by the young waitress's mother, given a room and told when breakfast would be served.

"Would it be alright if I sat in the common room there and visited with the other boarders, Ma'am?" he asked. "I'm not quite ready for bed yet."

"Certainly, Mr. Williams. You'll find my other boarders are friendly and love to talk," she said.

He took his carpetbag upstairs, freshened up a bit and walked back down. Three men were sitting in the living area, all talking amongst themselves. When he walked in, it got quiet.

"Hello. I'm James Williams," he said, smiling at each man in turn. "I'm here on business. Well, actually I was in Buffalo City on business but was brought here on the *Hattie Creef* for the night before my return to Elizabeth City and then on back to Richmond." He looked to see if the others would introduce themselves.

They sized him up and immediately saw an opportunity for some news from the outside world. All of them stood up, shook his hand and then invited him to take a seat and join them.

As he told them his story of setting up a glassworks in Buffalo City, they began to relax and get the picture that he was just a man like them who was out to make a living, all moral questions aside. He listened to their stories; they were all either fishermen or businessmen associated with fishing, and he asked them many questions. They were a font of information.

"So, as I said," Lucky began, "I'm still looking for that one good man to run my glassworks. I had high hopes for this fella named Virgil Timmons, but then I found that he had up and moved away from Buffalo City..." He shook his head sadly.

"Virgil?" a round faced man asked. "Virgil Timmons? Why, he's here in Ocracoke, working for Mr. Dows. In fact, he just married George Dows' oldest daughter... went to the weddin' myself."

"Really?" Lucky asked, brightening. "Do you think that I could talk to him, maybe convince him to move back to Buffalo City?"

All the heads moved as one from side to side. "Nope," the round faced man said, "Virgil's all set up here, done built himself a house and all. Doubt if he'd ever get that sweet lil' gal of his away from her ma and pa!" They all laughed and nodded.

"Too bad..." Lucky said, looking forlorn. "But still, I'd like to meet the young man with so fine a reputation as he has..."

One man brightened and said, "You can find him at the docks around dawn tomorrow. Look for the '*Coker Lass*' boat, she's the one his father-in-law operates. He'll be there."

After a few more minutes of friendly conversation about the locals Lucky said, "You men have been a pleasure to talk with, but I need to turn in now," getting up. "This is a lovely little island you've got here."

The group heartily agreed with his assessment and wished him a pleasant night's rest.

Up by dawn the next morning to catch the fishermen before they left, Lucky went walking around the lake looking for the *Coker Lass*. He spotted her: an older but substantial boat, with two men on deck preparing things for their departure. Waving at them, he shouted, "Morning! Nice day we're having for it today!"

The two men, both fairly young, looked up and waved back. "Little too early to tell," the nearest one responded, laughing. "I'll let you know after full light."

Lucky walked up the dock to the boat's side. "I'm looking for a man name of Virgil Timmons," he said, smiling at the two of them.

One of the young men began to slowly stand up, but the other froze and dropped the load he was carrying; it hit the deck with a loud clang. The first young fellow said, "And why would you be looking for Virgil?" The other fellow simply stood, mouth agape, staring at him, eyes wide open.

"Heard a lot of good things about him and wanted to offer him a job," Lucky called back.

The first young man turned to the second, who was still standing in place, but seemed to come alive when his friend asked, "Virgil? You want to talk to this man?"

Virgil's throat went dry. He couldn't believe that somebody had come here looking for him, much less to offer him a job. His heart automatically warned him it had something to do with the dead girls, but he tried to put that out of his head and look normal. He brushed his hands on the side of his worn pants and walked over to nearer where the man stood. The older man looked harmless, friendly enough, but wasn't that how they were supposed to look when they were searching for criminals?

"I got me a job already, Mister. Happy with it and don't want another," he said, waving him off and turning to go back to work.

"But it has to do with what's happening in Buffalo City, Virgil!" Lucky said.

Virgil froze again, his feet feeling like they were made of lead. Slowly he turned back, mumbled something to the other worker and jumped down up onto the dock. "Buffalo

City?   Is my Ma alright?" he asked, putting his fists on his hips.

"Your Ma?   I suppose, I don't know her, but I heard a little about her when I was there yesterday.   This is about something else..." Lucky glanced over toward the other young man and gave Virgil a raised-eyebrow look.

"I'll be back in ten minutes, Luther, I gotta find out what's goin' on in Buffalo City. If Mr. Dows gets back before I do, tell him it couldn't be helped," he said, turning to direct Lucky back along the dock towards the shore.   In ten long strides they touched land and he quickly turned to Lucky. "What's this about, anyway?"

Lucky smiled at him.   This was obviously a good kid, but he had the look of guilt written all over him. *Time for me to earn my money...*

"My name is James Williams.   I just came from Buffalo City," he said, extending his hand.

"Virgil Timmons," he finally responded, after looking at Lucky's hand for a long moment before deciding to shake it. "What do you want with me, Mr. Williams?"

"Like I said, I just came from Buffalo City..."

Virgil swallowed hard but said nothing.

"When I was there, I heard a lot about you..." Lucky said, watching Virgil's reaction closely.   The boy stood as still as stone, saying nothing, though a slight tick appeared under his left eye.

"I'm starting up a glassworks and looking for a man to run it for me. Everybody I talked to said that you were a hard-working, honest young man who would always be fair and treat everybody with respect. You have yourself a fine reputation, Son. That's the kind of man I'm looking for..."

Virgil exhaled loudly, averted his eyes and dropped his chin. "Like I said, I've got a good job."

"Would you consider moving back to Buffalo City for a lot more money than what you're making now?"

"No!" Virgil answered, a little too quickly and with definite certainty. "Absolutely not!"

Lucky gave him a quizzical look. "But you said your ma is there, and you being a newly married man, couldn't you use more money?"

Virgil squinted. "How'd you come to find out so much about me, Mister? You been askin' a lot of questions? There's a lot of good men in Buffalo City looking for work. *Why me*?" he said, taking a step forward.

Lucky held up his hands. "Hold on, Son, I don't mean anything by this, I just heard from a lot of people about what a good kid you were and since I had to lay over on Ocracoke for a night, I thought that I'd at least ask you if you'd be interested. You haven't even let me tell you about the job, and when I talked to Sasha and Ryan about you – "

"You talked to Sasha? Why would you want to be talking to him?" Virgil shot back.

"Well, he was at the tavern having some drinks when I was there, and he got my attention. I'd heard that you and he had worked together, so I thought I'd ask him what kind of worker you were…"

Virgil's face lost all color. "What did Sasha say about me?"

"Well, it was late and both of us had been drinking for a few hours already and…" Lucky paused, scratching his head as if to recall the exact conversation.

Virgil walked over to a nearby overturned bucket and sat down, putting his head in his hands. The color had drained from his face and he looked as if he might be sick or faint away.

"You alright, Virgil?" Lucky asked.

Wiping the sweat from his forehead, Virgil said, "I'm fine, just a little… overheated, I guess." He took a few deep breaths and then stood up again. "I worked with Sasha and Ryan for a while, but whatever they told you about me, good or bad, I wouldn't never work with the two of them again for love nor money. And I ain't interested in movin' back to Buffalo City for *any* reason, so I'll be going back to work now. Thank you very kindly for your offer." He turned and began to walk quickly down the dock back toward the boat.

Lucky panicked; he knew the kid was hiding something, but didn't know how to get it out of him. "It's really about those two girls, Virgil!" he called out.

Virgil froze again. Lucky found himself hoping that the poor kid would never have a job where he had to lie for a living because he'd starve to death. *Good thing he's becoming a fisherman*, he thought.

He turned back to Lucky slowly and said in a voice just above a whisper, "What two girls?"

Lucky walked up to him, put a hand on Virgil's shoulder and looked him in the eye. "I'm going to be honest with you, Virgil. I'm not actually here to offer you a job; I'm here because the father of two girls who've disappeared up in Elizabeth City has hired me to find out what has happened to his daughters. You're a married man now; you'll probably have your own little girls someday. Wouldn't you want to know what happened to them if they went missing?"

Virgil said nothing but his eyes flashed, full of pain.

Lucky went on. "I'm not with the police, like I said, I'm working for the girls' father. They still haven't turned up and he and his wife are worried sick. I've found what I believe to be a connection between moonshine runners and the girls' disappearance, and the more I look into it, the more I believe that the Russian Sasha and his partner Ryan are just the type of men who might do something like that. You were working for them back when it happened. Do you know something about them that might help me? Can you tell me *anything*?"

Lucky saw tears forming in Virgil's eyes. Virgil pulled away from him and turned toward the water, crossing his arms and looking out to sea. For several long minutes, Lucky let him stand there and think.

Finally, Virgil turned back and said, "I am not the kind of person who would ever hurt anybody, Mr. Williams, much less an innocent young girl. If I had done anything to those girls, I couldn't live with myself. But... Sasha and Ryan *are* the kind of men who don't care who they hurt, and they'd get rid of anybody who got in their way. That's all I can tell you about what you're asking me. I got me a wife now and a good family, and I cain't do nuthin' that would jeopardize that. I hope you believe me."

Lucky nodded, encouraging him to go on.

"So that's all I'm going to say about it," Virgil said. "If those girls ever – *turn up* – then you might be on the right track with your speculations..."

Lucky knew he had to press the kid. "Virgil, I believe you when you say that you wouldn't do anything like that. But I need to find out who might have, because the parents of those poor girls are going crazy with worry, wondering what might have happened to them. They *need* to know..."

Virgil stared at him and then swallowed hard. "Mister, I've done some thinkin' bout all that myself, and I believe that whoever took them girls ought to be punished. But there's some things that have to be left alone for the sake of everyone involved..."

Lucky could see that the young man wanted to tell him something, but was afraid for some reason. "Those girls were young and innocent, Virgil. They might have done something stupid, but certainly it was nothing that they deserved being killed for. I've got to find out what happened to them!"

Virgil shook his head. "That will never happen, Mr. Williams. But if Sasha and Ryan *were* involved and they knew that somebody had ratted them out, they'd kill the man who talked about it, and anybody he loved... They will never be convicted of killing those girls..."

Lucky reached out and grabbed the young man's upper arm. "But they need to pay for whatever they did, Virgil, can't you see that?"

Virgil got a hard look on his face, exhaled loudly and said, "I been givin' a lot of thought to that. Payin' for one murder is the same as paying for another – you can only be hung once. So if I was you, I'd look into something else that you might *could* prove: exactly where Sasha got that boat of his. There's two dead men's bodies hid out in the woods that nobody is looking for, as far as I know. That might get you the very evidence you need... and murder is a hangin' offense, whether it's a man or a girl been killed, right?"

Lucky looked confused. "Two dead **men**?"

Virgil nodded and pulled Lucky aside, talking quietly. "I found out about this long after it had happened or I wouldn't have ever got involved in that business hauling moonshine with 'em to begin with. The two of 'em got drunk one night and I overheard 'em laughing about it; it had something to do with stealing the boat from somebody who had just stolen it from the owner and then killin' the man. They committed murder to get that boat, Mr. Williams!"

"From what they said, the one man killed the original owner, left his body out in the woods, and then Sasha and Ryan to get the boat – got rid of the second one and buried him in the same place. But it was miles down from Buffalo City somewhere along the Alligator River, and they said nobody'd ever find 'em. They just laughed about it, like it was all a big joke," he said, rubbing his hand over his face and back through his hair. "After that, I knew I had to get away from 'em."

"And as to the other thing, the girls?" Lucky asked, knowing that pushing the kid could be risky but he had him here now and he was going to take advantage of that.

Virgil inhaled deeply and exhaled loudly. "I done said all I'm gonna say about that. I'm sorry, and if it would help you find those girls alive and healthy somewhere, I'd say more, but..." he shook his head slowly and sadly, giving Lucky a knowing look.

Lucky got a knot in his stomach. That was the one thing he'd expected, but dreaded to hear, and the last thing that he thought he'd ever hear Virgil say aloud. He nodded. "Thanks, Son, you've given me something to go on. I believe you when you say that you'd never hurt those girls, but if somebody else did, they've got to pay for it. You understand that, don't you?"

"I do. But my young wife suspects that she's already with child, Mr. Williams, and I cain't leave her now. If it was me that done it, I'd be man enough to pay, but it wasn't me, and she needs me now more than ever..." His eyes pleaded for compassion. "I cain't tell you no more 'bout that – I just cain't..."

"Virgil, I understand. I do. Let's say nothing of this conversation you and I have had today, both of us, alright? If what you told me about their boat gets those two convicted of murdering that man, then justice has been served when both of them hang. Let's hope we can prove it."

Nodding, Virgil looked up suddenly. "The boat – when they first brought it in, the name of it was the... '*Wilmington Woman*', before they painted over that and renamed it the *City Queen*. I didn't think nuthin' of it at the time, but if that might help you..."

Lucky smiled and patted him on the back. "That might just be the thing that hangs 'em, Son."

Virgil shook his hand. "Thanks, Mr. Williams, thank you so much, Sir..."

"The name is Lucky O'Rourke, but don't tell anybody please," he answered, grinning. "Up in Buffalo City I had to pass myself off as some kind of businessman from Richmond to get folks to talk to me. I have my own secrets to keep, you see. Now you go on back to work and don't worry about it. I'm sure that you'll hear the news if we are able to arrest Sasha and Ryan."

Virgil's shoulders fell and he slumped, putting his hands in his pockets. "I'm sure that I'll never *stop* worrying about it, Mr. O'Rourke, but that will be my burden to carry till the day I die and my punishment for not having said anything before this..."

Lucky nodded, waved and turned away. Tears came up in his eyes briefly, pain for the innocent young man who had been unlucky enough to get himself tangled up with the likes of Sasha and Ryan. He hoped with all his heart that he'd be able to keep the boy out of it, but he was going to do what had to be done...

Being a private detective was not a pleasant job some days.

Chapter 24

That afternoon after arriving back in Elizabeth City, Lucky got to work quickly. He went straight to the Sheriff's Office and asked if there were any reports of missing boats, large ones. Sheriff Graham reluctantly thumbed through a few papers and said, "Nope. Nothing recent."

"Go back a few months, Sheriff, if you please," Lucky said.

Amos Graham heaved a sigh and turned to pull out a folder with older notices in it. He thumbed through several, then looked up at Lucky. "And what's this got to do with those missing girls, O'Rourke?"

"I have a lead about some men down in Buffalo City, Sheriff, and I believe this missing boat is tied in with it somehow..."

The Sheriff gave a disgusted grunt and went back to rifling through the papers. After a few moments more, he stopped and looked up. "What was the name of that boat again?"

"The *Wilmington Woman*," O'Rourke answered. "I'm not sure of the owner's name, but I'm pretty sure about the name of the boat."

Amos looked up at Lucky. "Here's a report of a man named Josh Hillburn, who's been missing from down in

Wilmington for more'n eighteen months, and the name of his boat was…"

"Let me guess – the *Wilmington Woman*?"

"You think you're pretty smart, don't you, O'Rourke?" The Sheriff said, eyeing him suspiciously.

"Well, it's more that I'm just lucky – hence the nickname."

"Either way, here's what you're looking for," he said, handing Lucky the paper. "There's a description of both the man and the boat. Does it look like the one you're after?"

Lucky skimmed through the information. "I'd have to make a trip to Buffalo City to be sure, but what I'd like to do first is offer a reward for the discovery of the bodies of two murdered men down the river from there and then see what turns up…"

"**Two dead men**? What's that got to do with anything? And who's going to pay the reward?"

"Yes, **men**. And if we can find those two bodies, then that might just tie these people I'm investigating to the disappearance of the two girls."

"How exactly?" the Sheriff demanded.

"Well, at this point I can't say for sure, it's more just a hunch than anything…"

"And who's going to pay a reward for your *hunch*?" Amos scoffed.

Lucky smiled. "I might just do that myself, Sheriff, but I'll be letting you know. Can I keep this?" Lucky asked, holding up the flyer.

The Sheriff waved him away. "It's old and I haven't seen nor heard anything about it, so why not? But I tell you this, O'Rourke..." he gave him a piercing look, "if you turn up anything concrete, you let *me* know, you understand?"

"First thing I'd do would be to go to the law, Sheriff, you can be sure of that!" Lucky said, tipping his hat and turning to leave. "And thanks for the help!"

Sheriff Amos Graham propped his head on his fist and made a face. "That man is gonna be trouble," he said aloud. "I just hope that he's not stupid enough to try to cause trouble for me..."

Lucky's next stop was the Mercantile and Charlie Strout. "I've got a lead, Charlie," he said, after taking him aside. "But I need to post a reward for a missing boat and the bodies of two missing men. Can you help me with that?"

"*Missing men and a boat*? What's that got to do with my girls?"

"Well, I'm onto something that I think ties in with their disappearance, but I have to find two missing men's bodies south of Buffalo City to be sure. I know that it doesn't make sense now, but if you could trust me on this, I think it might actually help us to find out what happened to the girls..."

Charlie shook his head. "It makes no sense to me, but if you say it will help, then how much do you need?"

"How about fifty dollars?"

"Fifty dollars! That's half as much as I was offering for information to find the girls!"

Lucky nodded. "And it might lead us to finding out what's become of them. But, if you don't want to do it, Charlie, I understand. Let me just say this, though, before you decide: Knowing what happened to Rose and Linda will be worth it in the long run, no matter what we turn up. Having to live the rest of your life not knowing, it'll be really hard on you – and even harder on Mrs. Strout. I've seen this kind of thing before, and if you can find out one way or another, it's just better, is all I'm sayin'..."

Charlie ran his hand through his hair. He sighed and made a few other frustrated sounds. "Okay, you got your fifty dollars. But we need to find out something soon, Lucky; me and the missus – we're at our wits' end!"

Chapter 25

Two days later Lucky mailed out to Mrs. Needles a handful of flyers he'd had printed up. He attached a note that said he'd heard about this reward. He pointed out the offer for the return of the men's bodies from down the Alligator River and judiciously left out the part about the stolen boat. He added that he'd thought that some of the men in Buffalo City could maybe use the money.

She immediately spread the word and posted the flyers. The hunt was now on all along the Alligator River for the bodies of the two missing men, buried a few miles south of Buffalo City in the woods somewhere. Given only the scanty information in the flyer, the men of the area got their dogs and their shovels and set out in search of the graves. Wages of fifty cents a day was one thing; but fifty dollars in one shot got everybody in Buffalo City moving!

Lucky gave it three more days and then caught a ride on the *Hattie Creef* back to Buffalo City. He went straight to the hotel and checked in with Mrs. Needles.

"Why, Mr. Williams, so good to see you again!" she said, puffing out her chest. "It was very Christian of you to send those flyers down to us. What do you know about those missing men – were they murdered?" She stuck out her chin and scrunched up her face, hungry for any new rumors or gossip.

Shaking his head, Lucky said, "I'm afraid I don't know much, Mrs. Needles, I just saw the flyers and thought, since I had met the nice folks here, that perhaps some of them could find the bodies and make a little money for themselves." He shrugged. "Anything turn up yet?"

"No, but not for lack of trying, I'll tell you that! Fifty dollars is a whole lot of money these days, and folks here are desperate, so every man and his dog has been going down the river on skiffs and boats and rafts and anything else they can get to float. If there's somethin' to find, they'll find it, you can count on that!"

"I do hope so, Ma'am. I do hope so."

"Will you be staying long with us in Buffalo City this time?" she asked.

He shook his head. "Just overnight, I'm afraid. I need to take another look at a piece of property that might be exactly what I need, and then I'm off back to Richmond to finalize my plans."

She raised an eyebrow. "Which piece of land you looking at?"

He grinned. "Now, if I told you that, Mrs. Needles, the price of that property might just jump so high that I couldn't afford it, now, might'n it?"

She pressed her hand on her chest. "Why Mr. Williams, I'd never tell anybody anything, you know that!"

"Yes, I'm *sure* that's true, but let's just say that I like to keep my secrets under my hat." He leaned forward. "But you'll be the first one I tell once I've made my purchase!"

She batted her eyes at him. "Oh, how sweet! And you know that you can count on my discretion!"

"I fully appreciate the extent to which you can be trusted, Mrs. Needles!" He gave her his most charming smile and turned to leave.

Mrs. Needles smiled back at him and then looked confused and raised one eyebrow.

Lucky walked down to the docks about an hour before sunset. He chatted with a few of the fishermen he'd met before and, without revealing why, casually asked if anybody in these parts had a boat like the one described in the sheriff's report.

One old fella who hadn't been on a boat in years guffawed. "Oh, that sounds like the boat that the Russian uses to... well, ship his stuff on. I had me a boat like that years ago, a sweet one she was..." he got a dreamy look in his eyes. "That'n the Russian's got fer himself don't look like much, but you can believe me when I tell you that she fairly flies over the water! He's put a lot of money into that old gal, and now she purrs like a fat old cat!"

"And she's made him a whole lot of money, you know that," another old salt added, slapping his thigh and laughing so hard he spit on his companion. "Good money, I'm talking 'bout!"

"Uh-huh!" the first man agreed. "You said it!"

"Does he dock it around here?" Lucky asked.

The old sailor leaned forward. "Now, if it was anybody but you, Mr. Williams, I wouldn't never tell 'em, but between you and me, that boy and his friends will be some of your best customers for glass jugs. He keeps her tied up about a mile up the river," he added, nodding toward the south. "But if you go down there to talk business with him, you'd better be careful. He's got guns on that boat, and he ain't afraid to use 'em. I heard tell that he winged one of his own brothers who got too close and didn't let him know who it was that was comin'. So you be careful if you go down there!"

"Oh, no, I'd never go down there! It's only that I had heard about a boat like that over in Elizabeth City and wondered if there was any of them around here. It's a classic, you know, and I just wanted to take a gander at the old girl." He waved his hand. "Nope, I don't feel like walking a mile down the river anyway. Now then, ya'll tell me about the boats that you've been on in your life..." Lucky sat down and spent the next hour listening to all the tales that the two old fishermen could come up with about the boats that they'd worked on.

"Well, nice talking with you fellows, I'll be getting on back to the hotel now!" he said. Walking away, he was already making mental plans for his dawn excursion.

Before the sun came up, Lucky quietly sneaked out the back door of the hotel, dressed in his darkest pants and shirt. He walked quickly down to the docks and then headed south on the path that ran alongside the creek. Just as the sun was beginning to glimmer in the east, he came upon the Russian's boat. It was tied up exactly where the men had said, and there was no sign of life anywhere around it.

He sneaked down to the makeshift dock and looked around; there was nobody in sight. Quickly walking along the creek bank for the length of the boat, he examined it carefully, referring to some notes on a piece of paper that he'd brought along. It fit the description perfectly. And it was obvious that the old name had been painted over, but the new name was shorter and you could still make out the last four letters of 'woman' under the thin coat of white paint.

This was the missing boat, no doubt about it! He started back up the creek bank and toward the path. Just then a dog began to bark, and Lucky saw in the developing light that a house was not too far away from the water. He ran and took cover behind a big bush. At that same moment, the big blonde Russian stuck his head out the door and hollered something in Russian at the dog, which proceeded to bark even louder and point toward the bush where Lucky was hiding. The Russian stepped back inside, grabbed a rifle from just inside the door and came back out.

Looking around, Lucky realized that there was nothing else nearby for cover and that if Sasha came out, he'd have nowhere to go. The dog wouldn't stop barking and the big blonde man stomped over in his direction. He got as far as the dog and cursed, looked toward the boat and then kicked the dog hard in the ribs and said, "There is nothing out here, you stupid mutt! My head is hurting, and I told you to shut up!" The dog ran off around side of the house whimpering, and Sasha turned back, going inside and slamming the door behind him.

Lucky waited until all was quiet in the house and then ran for the nearest tree line. He hid behind a large live oak tree and then peeked toward the house. No sign of the dog or the Russian, so he took off and ran as fast as he could until his side hurt and he had to stop. By then, he was back near the docks, so he slowed to a walk and went back to the hotel, avoiding a few fishermen who were already up and at work.

He tiptoed quietly back into the hotel, up the back stairs and into his room, then fell face-first onto his bed. Realizing that he had discovered the whereabouts of the missing boat, now all he needed to tie the Russian to the missing men was the proof that the murders had taken place.

The men of Buffalo City knew these woods like nobody else. If those bodies were there, they had the skills and the monetary motivation to find them.

Late that very morning, Mrs. Needles ran into the hotel's common room screaming, "They found 'em! They found the bodies! It's a bloody mess I hear tell, but they found two men's bodies!"

He and all the other men jumped up and ran down to the docks. There, laid out on the weathered boards, were two lumps covered in sailcloth. Men were bustling all about and murmuring loudly. The man who had discovered the bodies and brought them in stood guard over them with his gun, and his dog was growling at anybody who got close, warning them to stay away.

Standing straight up, the man yelled, "I want all ya'll to witness the fact that it was me, Ezekiel Grandy, who brought these bodies in! Anybody here believe any different?"

"No, Zeke!"

"It's all your'n, Zeke!"

"Good job, Old Zeke!"

"What do they look like?"

"Have they been eaten by the bears and bobcats?"

"Let us see 'em!"

A general agreement went up on that last point, and Zeke begrudgingly pulled the sailcloth off first one body and then the next. A grisly sight met their eyes, but it had obviously been the bodies of two humans at one point.

Zeke stood up. "Some of the meat on 'em and some of their arms and legs is missing from critters gnawing on 'em, but the heads are still there, and even though they don't look like much, somebody might be able to recognize 'em," he said, then pulled the cloths back over the remains. "But it ain't purty, that's for sure!"

"Where'd you find 'em?"

"In a shallow grave 'bout five miles down the river! Old Bo here's the best trackin' dog in these parts!"

A general murmur of agreement went up from the crowd and Bo's glowing status as the best tracker in town was solidified by his amazing piece of work. One of the men even made Zeke an offer to buy Old Bo, but was turned down immediately.

Two of the town's leading men came forward. One was the mayor, who said, "Well, Ezekiel, we all agree that the reward is yours. But we need to git these bodies back to where they're supposed to go. Anybody know where that would be?" the taller one said, turning to the crowd.

Lucky stepped forward. "I believe the flyer said that would be Wilmington, Mr. Mayor. Is there a way to get the bodies there anytime soon?"

The two men conferred. "Well, no time soon, but we could send a telegraph message down to the lawmen at Wilmington," the Mayor said.

The crowd murmured its agreement. By general consensus, the bodies were wrapped up tight and moved to a storage shed outside the lumber office. A few men offered to stand guard during the night, and the people dispersed, except for the most curious who were still hoping to get another glimpse of the gory spectacle.

Lucky walked slowly back to the hotel. "Where can they send a telegram from here, Mrs. Needles?" he asked, when he saw her standing on the porch, straining her eyes toward the docks.

"What? Oh, yes, down at the post office, you can send one," she said, somewhat distracted by the melee going on as a small crowd began to gather around the shed holding the bodies. She pointed down the street.

He walked to the post office and found the two town leaders there discussing the situation.

"Excuse me, gentlemen, but when I was up in Elizabeth City I also saw a report about a missing boat that might be connected with those two bodies out there... here's a description of the boat and its owner." He handed the paper to the older of the two men.

The other one said, "What in the world does a missing boat in Elizabeth City have to do with those bodies?"

"Glory be, that's Sasha Sidorov's boat, or one just like it!" the older man said, rubbing his brow as he read the description. He shared a knowing look with the others.

"That would explain a lot about how those boys came by their boat, and that's somethin' we've all been wondering about!" the other replied. "I knew they didn't win it in no poker game!"

The two men looked at one another meaningfully and then walked off by themselves; they discussed the situation and made a decision, returning a few minutes later.

"Mr. Williams," the first man said, "if there is a connection between these two things then we need to keep it quiet so that crazy Russian don't run off. So, don't be tellin' nobody about this boat business, you hear?"

"Of course not, I wouldn't think of it!" Lucky answered. "Ya'll know the man – is it possible that the Russian could be somehow involved in this stolen boat and those murders?"

The two men nodded simultaneously. Then they telegraphed the Wilmington Police Department that two bodies had been found and the missing boat, the *Wilmington Woman* was possibly docked in Buffalo City. Since Buffalo City had no police, they swore Lucky and the telegraph man to secrecy. All of them knew that the Russian and his friend were dangerous and none of them wanted to tangle with them personally. And if Sasha found out that he was even under suspicion, he'd run off and be gone without a trace.

By the next morning the New Hanover County Sheriff and several of his men had arrived by Coast Guard boat. They went first to examine the bodies and, comparing them with the description of the missing boat owner, Josh Hillburn, felt fairly sure that one of them had been the man. He'd obviously been shot through the heart.

One of the deputies pointed toward the other body and said, "Sheriff, that other one there kinda looks likes that

Turner fellow we had locked up for a time last year… think it could be him? Nobody's reported him missin', but then nobody would miss the likes of him!"

The Sheriff looked carefully. "I believe you're right, Bill! Wonder what he was doin' up this way with Hillburn?"

Lucky went over with the town leaders and mentioned to the Sheriff that he had his suspicions that these murdered men were somehow related to the disappearance of the two girls up in Elizabeth City.

"How would you know anything about that?" the Sheriff asked him.

"Let's just say it's a hunch, Sheriff. I'm a private detective and I've been digging into the disappearance of those girls and Buffalo City moonshine keeps coming up. Just ask Sasha and Ryan if they know anything about those girls, that's all… then see what they say."

The Sheriff thought it over and nodded. "When we question them, I'll bring it up. With no evidence of course, all I can do is ask, but I promise you that I will do that – and I *know* how to question a man. I heard about those girls and it makes me sick that something like that could have happened around here!"

"What makes you think the two things are connected, mister?" the Sheriff asked, giving him a look.

Lucky scratched his head. "I got some information from an anonymous source that the two of them were connected to those girls. It sounded credible enough, and if they murdered a couple of men, what's to stop them from abducting the girls?"

The Sheriff looked at Lucky and raised an eyebrow. "An anonymous source, you say? Well, like I said, I'll be sure to bring it up. Did they ever find those girls, do you know?"

Lucky shook his head. "No. And their parents are sick with worry; they need to find out something, one way or another..."

"I understand," he said. "I been a lawman for thirty years, and I have seen that it is better if you know, even if it's something you don't want to find out."

Lucky nodded. "Yes, Sheriff, you're right about that."

Afterward, they gathered some more local men and the group quietly made their way down the river path to where Sasha's boat was still tied up. The Sheriff walked out onto the creek bank where a few planks were thrown down to access the boat. He stopped short and put up his hands when he heard someone on board yell out, "Hold it right there, or I vill shoot you!"

"I'm just here to ask you some questions, that's all..." the Sheriff said, standing perfectly still.

"And who vould you be?"

"I'm the Sheriff of New Hanover County and I need to ask a couple of questions about some bodies we've found and the ownership of this here boat."

"Yes, I saw that flyer but that's got nothing to do with us!" Sasha called out.

"You had better stay back, you got no business on our boat! This is our boat!" Lucky recognized the voice of Ryan coming from the cabin.

"I got every right to come aboard that boat and ask for proof of ownership, and if you've got nuthin' to hide, then you'll show it to me!"

After about thirty seconds of silence, Sasha called out, "Vell, I don't see no badge on you, so you might not be vhat you say you are! Go away and leave us alone!"

The Sheriff reached into his shirt pocket for his badge. Seeing his movement, Ryan shot a warning shot at his feet. "Stand still," he hollered, moving up to stand beside Sasha. Both of them were aiming rifles at the sheriff.

"You boys don't realize what you're doin'," the Sheriff yelled. "It's a federal offense to shoot at a law officer! Put those guns down right now!"

Sasha mumbled something to Ryan, who moved quickly to cast off their moorings and then ran to the wheelhouse to start the engine.

"Stop it right there!" the sheriff yelled.

"Ryan, get her going!" Sasha hollered.

As the sound of the engine fired up, the Sheriff took two steps back. "Fire!" he yelled, and then he dropped down to hit the dirt.

The sound of gunfire rang out from the trees and Sasha immediately collapsed to the deck of the ship, his eyes full of shock. Ryan ran out of the wheelhouse and was taken down by a shot to his right thigh but held onto his gun as he fell.

The Sheriff and his men ran toward the boat. Two of them secured the moorings and the Sheriff yelled, "Surrender in the name of the law! We know you stole this boat!" He looked over toward Lucky. "And we know about those two girls in Elizabeth City, too!" he yelled loudly.

Ryan pulled himself up and aimed the rifle. "Them girls was an accident, you hear me, we didn't mean to kill 'em, it was just an accident!"

The Sheriff looked over at Lucky and nodded. "But they're dead anyway, aren't they, and you're the ones who done it and who'll hang for it!"

Ryan croaked, "They're dead but I ain't gonna hang for nuthin'! You'll never take me alive!" He took a shot at the sheriff and hit him in the upper arm. Immediately several men ran up to the boat, shot Ryan dead, and then decided to put two more into Sasha for good measure.

"Save the cost of a trial," one of them muttered, kicking the bodies to make sure that there was no life left in either of them. "Murderers and probably rapists, too! Don't deserve a trial!" Then he spit on the bodies.

The group boarded the boat and drove it on up to Buffalo City, where it docked. The Hanover County Sheriff was taken to the local doctor, who pronounced him "grazed," patched him up and sent him on his way. After the Sheriff was treated and the boat secured, telegrams were sent to both Elizabeth City and Wilmington. More law officers from both places were sent for, to appear as soon as possible.

Later that day, Sheriff Amos Graham came riding up on a Coast Guard boat. He was directed to the Buffalo City town hall, where he found the Hanover County Sheriff resting, consulting with his men. Lucky was hanging back, watching it all from the shadows.

Amos barged into the conversation. "And what do you think all this killin' and boat stealin' has to do with us?" Graham demanded of the other sheriff.

"Well, if you'll tell me who you are, I might just answer that." He shifted his arm in the sling so that the pain was not so bad.

Amos held up a piece of paper. "I'm Sheriff Amos Graham from Elizabeth City. I got this telegram to get here as soon as possible and here I am. What's all this about and who are you?" he asked in a threatening tone.

"I'm Hanover County Sheriff Bill Payton. Sit down, Graham, and I'll tell you."

Sheriff Graham begrudgingly complied.

"You know those two girls missing from your town?" Payton asked.

"Of course, no sign of 'em yet."

"Well, these two men we just killed, they murdered the owner of a boat, stole his boat and when we confronted them about those two girls up in Elizabeth City, they said, 'They're dead, it was an accident, we didn't mean to kill them girls, and you're not taking me to jail.' That was all we got out of them, and then we had to kill 'em in self-defense. That was as good as a confession in my book, so I'm sorry to say that I suspect those two girls are dead as well. Has anything related to their disappearance turned up yet?"

Sheriff Graham sat still for a while. He really had not believed that the girls were dead, but thought they'd simply run off. Facing these new facts, he lowered his chin and said quietly, "Nope, not yet, not a trace of 'em."

"I didn't have time to question them properly because they came out shooting, but I imagine that if they didn't mind killing two men then killing two girls wouldn't bother 'em, neither. And like I said, that one seemed to know just what I was talking about, but claimed it was some kind of accident."

His deputy snorted. "Accident, huh! Them two low-lifes murdered them girls, sure as shootin'!"

"Well, if we find their bodies..." Amos began.

"Yes, *if you find their bodies*, then we can tie all this together and figure out what happened maybe. But let me tell you, I have no doubt that whatever happened to those two girls, these two men we just killed had something awful to do with it. I'm taking these bodies and the stolen boat back to Wilmington. If I get any more information, I'll telegraph you."

"Oh, Lord, I do hope they're not dead..." Sheriff Graham said. "They were just little girls..." He buried his face in his hands and sat quietly for several seconds. Then he lifted his face and added, "And if we do find 'em, I'll be sure to let ya'll down in Wilmington know, Sheriff..."

Lucky listened to all this and slipped away. The case had been solved as far as he was concerned; but the hardest part for him was yet to come.

Chapter 26

Lucky caught a ride back to Elizabeth City on the Coast Guard boat. Amos avoided him for the whole trip, and seemed to be in a mood that might even be considered regretful. Once back in town, Lucky asked the Sheriff, "Well, do you want to tell Charlie or do you want me to do it?"

Shaking his head, Amos said, "I sure don't want to do it, so if you're willin', then the job is yours."

Lucky nodded and headed off toward the Mercantile. Taking Charlie into the back room, Lucky told him the whole story of the missing boat, the two dead men and what had happened there on the creek bank below Buffalo City.

Charlie looked off into space and asked, "So, they as good as admitted it, then? Do you have any doubts yourself?"

Lucky shook his head. "No, and the Sheriff from Wilmington said that what Ryan said was a confession in his book. So, I'm very sorry to have to tell you that the girls are probably dead, Charlie." He put his hand on the man's shoulder briefly. "I had hoped it would end differently..."

Tears streamed down Charlie's face as the full impact of the situation hit him. "So, we'll probably never find their bodies and know for sure, then... Nelda is gonna be so tore up by all this that she might die herself!" He turned his head away and covered his face with both hands.

Charlie stood up, mumbled, "I'll talk to you later, Charlie..." and made his way out into the store to give the man some privacy. He told young Freddy that they should close up, gave him the basic facts and watched as the young man's face contorted and his tears began to fall. "I'll walk over with you," Lucky added, taking the boy by the arm and walking him to the front door. Lucky turned the 'Open' sign around so that the 'Closed' side showed, and then he pulled down the shade. "Lock the door behind me, Freddy," he said to the whimpering young man, who nodded and did as he was told.

Back out on the street, all Lucky could think about was Helen. He wanted to be the one to tell her and to thank her for the help she'd given him; it would only be right. At least that's what he told himself as his feet took him down to her tavern without slowing down.

She looked up at him from the bar and smiled, but then saw the look on his face. She ran over to him, grabbed him by the upper arms and said, "What is it, Lucky? Did you find the girls?"

He shook his head from side to side slowly, but then changed and began to nod. She directed him to a seat and poured him a drink. "Tell me what happened, Lucky..."

He stared at the glass, lifted it and downed the two fingers of Buffalo City moonshine in one gulp, coughing and sputtering as tears came to his eyes. "Strong stuff..." he said, making an excuse and wiping his eyes.

She nodded and waited.

He took several deep breaths and then began to tell her the story of what had happened since the last time he'd seen her, managing to omit the part about Virgil's implied involvement. Somehow in telling Helen the details, he began to let the full emotional impact of it all settle into his heart and mind and before he knew it, he was wiping more tears from his cheeks, trying hard but unsuccessfully to stop the flow of tears.

"Oh, Lucky," she said, patting his forearm, "it's a terrible thing, but look what you've done – you've found out what happened to the girls and brought the guilty ones to justice!"

"Somehow..." he said, "that is never enough, Helen. When a case ends badly like this, I have to ask myself if I want to stay in this line of work..."

She slapped the table, jarring him back to reality. "Of course you do! If it hadn't been for you, those two men's bodies would have never been found, the guilty men would still be running around free and Charlie and Nelda would never know what had happened to their girls! It's the worst possible news, yes, but don't you think that it's better for them than never knowing, always wondering and worrying?"

He focused on her beautiful face. "Yes, you're right, Helen... but right now I don't want to think about any more cases, I just want to forget!"

She poured him two more fingers of rye whiskey. "Don't leave town just yet, Lucky. Stay a few more days and spend some time with me. I'll close the tavern and we'll go up the river and go fishing or do something else to take your mind off all this."

He pulled himself together emotionally, lifted his shoulders, looked at her and smiled weakly. "Helen, you know just what to say to a man... How do you do that? Years of tending bar?"

"Hummffff! More like a lifetime of being a woman, Lucky O'Rourke!"

"And a smart, beautiful one at that!" he said. Taking her hand, he pulled it up to his lips and kissed it gently. "Thank you for being you, and for being my friend."

She smiled. *Maybe he wasn't such a schmuck after all...*

"I need to make a trip down to Ocracoke, Helen. And when I get back, then the two of us can spend some time together. How does that sound?"

She looked puzzled but said, "There's a boat that goes out down that way in about an hour or so, if you hurry you can make it on that one. More than likely you'll have to spend the night there, but you could be back here tomorrow..."

He nodded and stood up. "Alright then, that's what I'll do. Please don't say anything to anyone about where I've gone, Helen, if anyone thinks to ask you about it. Would you do that for me?"

"Of course, Lucky. Just come back to me safe and sound, you hear?"

He smiled, his heart lifting from the heaviness that had weighed it down. She had asked him to come back *to her*! "You bet, Helen, safe and sound!"

By the time Lucky had made it to Ocracoke, it was late in the day. He asked for directions and made his way to Virgil Timmon's house. Virgil was sitting outside under a tree, peeling some apples, but stood up and immediately went as white as a sheet when he saw Lucky. He dropped the apple he was holding.

"Hello, Virgil…"

Virgil swallowed hard. "Mr. O'Rourke. What brings you back here to Ocracoke?"

Lucky took a seat in the chair beside Virgil. "Can we talk for a while, Son?"

Virgil nodded and sat down.

"First, I wanted to tell you that we caught the men who stole the boat and murdered the man who owned it. Turned out to be Sasha and Ryan, you were right about that. Thank you for helping us to track them down."

Virgil nodded absentmindedly. "And the other...?"

"Well, Sasha and Ryan as good as admitted that they killed those girls, claiming that it was an accident, but then they started shootin' and the Hanover County Sheriff and his boys had to shoot 'em dead. So, everyone assumes it was them that took 'em and that the girls are dead... At least their parents know now..."

Virgil's hand flew to cover his eyes and he made a choking sound. After a minute or so, he took a deep breath. "So, Sasha and Ryan – they're both dead?"

Lucky nodded. "And dead men don't talk."

Virgil reached over and put his hand on Lucky's shoulder. "Then do you think justice has been served?"

"Yes, I'm satisfied it has. How about you?"

Virgil thought about it. "They needed to pay for what they did, and I reckon that they have paid the price, so now what happens to 'em is up to God." He looked at Lucky. "Would you care to come in and have supper with us, Mr. O'Rourke? My Lillian is a fine cook, and there's always plenty to go around..."

Lucky considered it. "Are you sure, Virgil? Who would you tell her that I am?"

Virgil nodded. "You're a friend of mine, Lucky. That's all she needs to know. And you're welcome to stay the night if you want. I built that little shed over there for my mother, but she's not comin' to live with us. There's a bed and all in there that you can use."

"Is your mother alright, then? Nothing's happened to her, has it?"

Virgil got a crooked grin on his face. "No, well, yes... what I mean to say is she's fine and she got married again so that she could stay in Buffalo City."

"Married?" Lucky was as surprised as he sounded, after all he'd heard about the woman.

"Yep. There's a serious shortage of women in Buffalo City, and one of the old codgers there decided that he was man enough to take her on in exchange for somebody to cook and clean for him, I reckon..." Virgil tried to suppress a laugh, but wound up choking and then burst out laughing.

Lucky raised both eyebrows but said nothing.

"And that's just fine with me and Lillian! You wouldn't believe how much more peaceful my life is these days!"

Lucky smiled and nodded. "And now you can rest easy on another account. No more needs to ever be said about anything that's happened as far as the murders go, Virgil, and you can put it all behind you."

Virgil got a very serious look on his face. "I might be done with that part of my past, Lucky, but I don't think it'll ever be done with me... Well, no matter, let's go inside and see what that purty lil' gal of mine's puttin' on the table."

"I'd be delighted, Virgil. You say her name is Lillian?" he said as they both rose and headed for the house.

"Yep. But I always call her my Sweet Lil, cause that's what she is to me!"

Lucky headed back to Elizabeth City the next morning on the same supply boat that he'd come in on. After checking in with the Sheriff to make sure that everything was all tied up, he headed for Helen's place.

She was closed, but was already in there getting ready for the afternoon and evening's work. When he tapped on the window and she saw that it was him, she ran over and flung open the door, stopping just short of throwing her arms around him. He grinned.

"Your trip to Ocracoke — you got done what you needed to do?" she asked.

"Yep. Now I'm all yours for as long as you want me!"

She crossed her arms and looked him up and down. "I never said that I wanted you for *any* length of time, Lucky O'Rourke, but if you can behave yourself, I might consider taking the day off..."

"Yes, Ma'am! I promise to be good. You said something about taking me fishing, I believe..."

She smiled. "Let me make the arrangements with Joe, and then we'll get going. I've got a little cabin down the river a ways. We can take my boat and head down there for the day."

"You've got a boat? And a cabin?"

She nodded. "There's a lot about me that you don't know, Lucky. But if you're interested, I can spend a little time filling you in..."

"How thirty does or forty years sound to you?" he asked, grinning.

"You're gettin' a little ahead of yourself, Mr. O'Rourke, but I'll tell you this: I will give you the rest of the day today and then we'll take it one day at a time. How does that sound?" She tossed her hair back and challenged him with a look.

He walked up and put his arms around her, drawing her close. Staring down into those deadly dangerous blue eyes, he said, "One day at a time is all I will ever ask from you, Helen." Then he kissed her so soundly that she didn't have time to give him any sass.

Chapter 27

Two days later Zed Freeman was chugging toward home with his measly catch of the day. Some days were good, some were bad; it was the way of fishing and he knew it all too well. Suddenly he caught sight of something large floating in the water. Slowing the boat to a crawl, he pulled up beside it and cursed.

"No, God, no, please!" he said, reaching for a grappling hook. He snagged the rope holding the two bodies together. As he hauled them up onto the deck, his first thought was of his own children. The girls lay there, bound together like Siamese twins, and even though they'd been in the water a long time it was easy to tell who it was – who it had to be. The rope holding the two of them together had a frayed end – a piece that looked like it might have been tied to something else.

Zed ran to the other side of the boat and threw up. Then he began to cry like a baby. He'd seen some awful things in his life, but nothing as devastating as this. Eventually he managed to pull himself together and cover the bodies with a tarp. The rest of the way in he prayed for Charlie and his family.

Charlie and Nelda got to say goodbye to their girls at last; they had an extra-large casket constructed and buried them together, side-by-side, just as they'd been found.

Elizabeth City was shaken to its core by the horrible tragedy, and the moonshine trade slowed down considerably after that discovery. The good people of the town decided by silent agreement that there were other, better ways to bring money into their port town.

A reporter came down from Norfolk and wrote a long story about the crime. Interviewing all the local folk, he decided that he needed to talk to Lucky O'Rourke, who seemed to be the key man in bringing the culprits down. He hunted him up in Norfolk and met him at his office. Lucky gave him the facts in as dignified a manner as possible. When the reporter asked how he managed to connect the murders of the two men and the missing boat to the girls from Elizabeth City, Lucky shook his head.

"No. I won't reveal that source of information for obvious reasons. It was a tip from an observant person, somebody who asked to remain nameless and so I shall do just that!" He raised an eyebrow at the reporter. "And if you expect me to give you permission to use my story, then you will do the same."

Despite further prying, that was all the reporter could get out of him.

When the reporter's story broke in the *Virginia-Pilot*, the headline on the front of the paper proclaimed in bold letters, *"The Buffalo City Moonshine Murders"*. It sold more copies than any edition to date.

Sheriff Amos Graham quit not long afterward and moved to somewhere down in South Carolina.

Lucky and Helen got their fishing trip; that led to many more such trips and every chance he got Lucky was driving down to Elizabeth City to spend time with Helen. One evening as they sat outside overlooking the docks, he asked her, "So, how did you come to own a bar, Helen?"

She looked away. "When I was sixteen my father decided that I needed to be married; so he found a man, a good man who'd lost his young wife to a fever, and arranged it all. Abe was a fine man and he was good to me; I was just a kid and figured that I was lucky to be married to a man who was settled and had his own home and boat. We had a son together, Jonah. He was the light of my life..."

Lucky frowned. He didn't like that she had used the past tense with regard to her boy.

"One day," she continued, "they both went out on the boat. Jonah was only twelve but he insisted on going with his father whenever Abe would let him. That day a nasty squall came up unexpectedly and the boat was lost together with all hands. No bodies were ever found, but that was ten years ago and we lost hope after a short while."

"I'm so sorry, Helen," Lucky said, taking her hand.

"Thank you, Lucky. I was buried in grief for months, but then my uncle Samuel asked me to come and help him here at his bar during the day with some cooking and a few other things. It's never been a rowdy place, and many of the patrons bring their wives in here for a drink or a bite to eat. So I did it, against my father's wishes, but I had to find something to do with myself, Lucky, I was going crazy..."

He nodded and squeezed her hand.

"After a few months, I began to feel alive again. The friendly people who came in here were all so good to me, and Uncle Samuel, he made me feel useful again, like I was still good for something... Eventually I started working later in the day... he taught me bartending and how to run the place. Uncle Sam died two years ago and left the bar to me. That's how I became a female bar owner..." She looked at him, shrugged and grinned. "It saved my life, literally."

"Did your father ever accept it?"

She nodded. "Oh, yes. After a while he came around to the idea, and he would often come in here himself and have a beer or lend a hand. My mother could never bring herself to come here, but she never disparaged me for it. In fact, she encouraged me because she saw how good it was for me. Right up until they died, both of them were my biggest supporters..." Tears glistened in her beautiful blue eyes.

"Oh, Helen, it must have been so hard for you to lose your husband and son at the same time... I can't imagine..."

She wiped her eyes. "Yes, it was, especially Jonah... I don't think that I'd ever truly loved anyone until my son came along..."

Lucky nodded. "You were very young when you married."

"Too young! But I didn't know it at the time and tried to do the best I could as a wife and mother. Abe was a good man, and he treated me well, but what I felt for him was more... respect than love, really."

"And you never had the desire to remarry?"

She shook her head. "It would take a special kind of man to turn my head at this point in my life," she said, grinning at him. "I'm quite well off materially and have a lot of friends," she added, waving her arm around. "Most of the men who've shown interest in me are widowers who want me to give it all up and keep house for them and their passel of children; either that or they need my money. I'm simply too independent now, I guess, but I don't think I could live with someone dictating my every move again." She shrugged and smiled at him, an impish grin that made her eyes dance.

He nodded and said, "I can understand. My life has been unconventional as well, what with all the traveling I've had to do. I almost got married when I was a policeman in Baltimore, but the lady got a better offer and wasn't interested in living on a cop's salary, I guess. After that, I just never seemed to have the time or energy to invest in a serious relationship." He looked at her and grinned himself. "I'm a little too independent myself, you see!"

Helen realized that they were holding hands, but decided that was fine with her. This man was different; he liked her just the way she was, and he didn't seem to want to change her. She let herself enjoy the comfort of his strong hand.

Virgil and Lillian had seven children, four of them boys who went into the fishing business with their father, and then later the sport-fishing guide business during the 50's and 60's. All of the children were still alive when their father died, and a large group of his grandchildren came from various places in the South to attend his funeral. One of his granddaughters still lived on Ocracoke Island when Sarah found the message in a bottle.

Chapter 28

Ocracoke Island
Present Day

After doing more research on the internet for what felt like hours, Sarah closed her computer and rubbed her shoulders. There was little to nothing to be found about Buffalo City and two missing girls. She leaned over her laptop, put her head in her hands and shut her eyes. *There had to be more to it.* It was a long time ago, true, but something as rare as two young girls being killed would not have gone unreported, especially in the 1930's.

Suddenly her head shot up as she remembered Virgil's reference to the Pasquotank River. She googled that name and discovered that this river was the main water access to Elizabeth City, North Carolina. So, putting it all together, she searched, "Elizabeth City, NC, missing girls, 1930's".

After all the hotel and restaurant recommendations for the area, further down the page she saw a reference to an old article in the *Virginia-Pilot* entitled, "The Buffalo City Moonshine Murders." She sat up straight, clicked on the link and scrolled through what looked like a photocopy of the front page of an old newspaper, probably scanned into the internet records by some vigilant local historian.

Pouring through the facts, she read that two girls, sisters from Elizabeth City had been brutally murdered. Their bodies were eventually recovered from the river and the town had been shocked.

An investigator named Lucky O'Rourke was quoted, as was the sheriff in Elizabeth City (one Amos Graham), along with several of the townspeople who willingly gave their opinions and speculations about what had happened to the missing girls.

O'Rourke said that the murderers, two men who had confessed in a roundabout way when questioned for stealing a boat and committing two other murders, had been killed in a firefight down in Buffalo City several weeks after the disappearance of the girls. One of the murderers was named as Sasha Sidorov.

The reporter had enlivened the story with hearsay and conjecture, a staple of the day. But there was no mention in the article of a Virgil Timmons. However, there was one reference to what the reporter called 'an anonymous source' who gave a solid tip to O'Rourke that helped him to put the pieces together and track down the murderers.

Could that anonymous source have been Virgil Timmons? No reference to Virgil came up in a search with regard to Elizabeth City, but it had to be! No one else could have known about the crime, could they? Sarah took her computer out onto the back porch and shared it all with Kate and Aleta.

"So what we have here," Kate said, pointing toward the bottle and the message that lay beside it, "is the confession of a man who was somehow involved in the murders but was never charged with the crime – someone who helped the detective solve it and bring the culprits to justice, but was then never connected with it afterwards."

"Someone," Aleta added, "who carried the burden of the girls' murder on his conscience all the days of his life, and at the end he had to put it down on paper and toss it into the Albemarle Sound..." She shook her head.

Sarah sighed heavily and rubbed her face. She looked up at the other two and said, "So, here we are back at the beginning. What do we do with this information?"

"Could Virgil have any family left here in Ocracoke?" Kate asked.

"And if he does..." Aleta put in, "would we want to be the bearers of such news? How would you like to find out that your father or grandfather, who you always thought of as a wonderful old man, was involved with a grisly murder?"

"Oh, no!" Kate said, putting her fingers over her mouth and shaking her head. "We couldn't do that, not to anybody! It wasn't Virgil's fault!"

The three of them agreed without any more discussion that the best thing to do was simply to let it lay, to keep it between them and not tell anyone else, not even their own families. Sarah put the paper message in a ziplock bag and put it and the bottle away in her suitcase. She would keep it as a reminder of an exciting trip to Ocracoke and a memory of a man that she now felt she knew well, but would never meet.

The next day, Sarah went to the realty office to make sure that all the paperwork was in order for them to check out two days later.

"Which cottage are you in, again?" the lady at the computer asked.

"The one on Silver Lake Drive, down toward the end, with the good view of the lighthouse off the back porch," Sarah said, pulling the paperwork out of her bag to check the name of the cottage.

The woman glanced at the papers and gave her an enigmatic smile. "Oh, you mean 'Sweet *Lil's House*'? That's one of our most popular cottages. Let's see... yes, you're all paid up and all you have to do is drop off the package of paperwork, together with the keys, in the drop-box outside on the porch. We hope you'll come back again to our little island!" she said, in a smiling, friendly manner. "We love our visitors!"

"I'm sure that we will, we come every year; it's a tradition that the three of us girlfriends have kept up for over ten years now," Sarah said, getting her things together to leave. "Thanks for everything," she said, turning and waving goodbye as she headed to the door.

Stopping with her hand on the doorknob, Sarah turned back and asked the lady, "What did you say the name of the cottage was?"

"That's *'Sweet Lil's House,'*" she answered.

Sarah walked back up to the counter; she had rented it herself but not made the connection. "Interesting name. Do you know anything of the history of the place?"

The lady lit up, smiling. "Of course I do, it was my grandmother's house! It was originally built for her by my Grandpa Virgil back in the 30's, I believe. It's been added onto and remodeled, updated and all that, but the front four rooms make up the basic house that they started with way back then. It's been in my family for all these years, and it's special to us. We have our family gatherings there in the off-season, and all us grandkids bring our children there and tell them the story of how our Grandpa loved our Grandma so much that he moved from Buffalo City, built her a house, and never left the island!"

"Virgil? His name was Virgil?" Sarah blinked her eyes.

"Yes, Virgil Timmons. He ran a successful fishing business till somewhere up in the 1970's or so. Then he got too old and had to retire. Grandma Lillian died first, and then he died back in the early 80's. But they were two of the town's most beloved characters. It was said about my grandfather that he 'never spoke an ill word of anybody' and that he was a generous, caring man who helped out everyone in the community." She smiled widely, obviously proud of her heritage. "Would you like to see a picture of him?"

Sarah nodded. "Please!"

The lady walked over to a desk and picked up an old photo in a frame. "This is Grandpa Virgil," she said proudly, handing the picture over to Sarah. "He was a handsome man, don't you think?" She was smiling from ear to ear.

The man in the picture was wearing a pinstripe suit and tie and looked to be in his forties. His fedora was tipped rakishly to one side and his strong jaw, full lips and the shadow of a beard gave him a ruggedly handsome appearance. The look on his face was one of mild amusement, lending him a look of kindness. Sarah smiled as she studied the photo.

"Yes, he's very handsome! What was he like?" Sarah asked, still looking at the man's face.

"Grandpa Virgil? Oh, he was just the nicest man you would ever want to meet! He loved all of his kids and grandkids so much – he was usually holding one of the little ones on his lap. He had a soft voice and an easy laugh, and the way he loved my grandmother..." Her eyes got a little misty. "Well, he always called her his Sweet Lil, and that's what everybody on the island came to call her eventually. It was Virgil and Sweet Lil, and anyone who knew them would tell you that they were the best kind of people! Of course, they were my grandparents, so I can tell you that truthfully because I knew them."

"All you have to do is ask any of the old folks on this island," she continued, "and they'll tell you what an amazing man Grandpa was. He would help out anyone and everyone, and spent most of his money on other people who would need it. And Grandma Lil was right there beside him, helping him do it! I wish you could have known them..."

"Me, too," Sarah said, her eyes getting misty. She handed the photo back to the woman. "Thank you for sharing that with me. It means more than you could ever know."

The woman gave her a puzzled look and said, "I do hope that you'll be returning to visit us here on Ocracoke someday."

"Well, we will definitely be back next year," Sarah said, smiling. "And we'll be sure to reserve early so that we can get 'Sweet Lil's House'. I think that's where we'll be staying every year from now on!"

The lady at the desk grinned. "Everyone who stays there seems to love the place! It's full of our family history, and a lot of that history nobody ever finds out about!"

"Yes, I'm sure about that..." Sarah said, smiling. "Nice to meet you and we'll look forward to seeing you next year!"

She walked back out to her car, put her purse in the seat beside her, buckled her seat belt and put her hands together on the steering wheel. She leaned her head down against her hands.

Now, she thought, *the circle is complete; the mystery is solved. Virgil turned out to be a fine man after all!*

Sarah drove slowly down the winding road toward the cottage; she was full of happiness, relief and a wonderful 'rest of the story' to tell her friends. And to think that *she* had been the one who'd found Virgil's message in a bottle!

What a sweet serendipity... she thought. *Hey, that sounds like a good title for one of Kate's novels...*

Sarah laughed out loud, stuck her arm out of the window and felt the seabreezes blowing away the rest of her anxieties. Yes, this vacation had been just what she'd needed – and more!

The End

Ocracoke Island today is a charming, peaceful village that entertains tourists in the Outer Banks and offers them a restful vacation in a place that time seems to have forgotten. The people, shops and restaurants there offer truly unique and special enjoyments.

If you can go to Ocracoke for a short visit, leave your troubles on the ferry when you pull out of Hatteras and don't pick them up again until you get back – or maybe even not then...

And if I'm down there with 'Aleta' and 'Sarah' starting a new novel, be sure to say hello!

Buffalo City was a typical turn-of-the-twentieth-century backwoods town. The people who lived there were rough and hardy, and they enjoyed a simple life. It was a time when neighbors gathered together, entertainment was simple and free, and people were more important than things.

The surviving residents who had lived there (when interviewed) all expressed a longing for the kind of life they lived in that simpler time. Perhaps there is a lesson in that for all of us of in this complicated, modern, hurry-up age.

And while the story of Virgil Timmons is fiction, I did hear a good tale from there about two brothers who loved the same woman and wound up killing her accidentally and feeding her body to the alligators... But I'm pretty sure that was fiction, too...

Sharron Frink

If you have enjoyed this or any of my other novels, I'd like to ask you to please go to amazon.com and leave a review there so that others will know your thoughts on this book.

Feel free to contact me through my website, *sharronfrink.com*, with any comments you might have – I love to hear from my readers!

Thanks so much for taking the time (I do realize that you *didn't have to*, you know...) to read my books! I sincerely hope that you have enjoyed them!

16560715R00154

Made in the USA
Middletown, DE
18 December 2014